# SWIFT MISSION

Also by Brian D. Cornett:

Tales From The Brass Rail
ISBN 0-9720640-4-4
*A collection of short stories*

# SWIFT MISSION

BRIAN CORNETT

iUniverse, Inc.
Bloomington

# Swift Mission

iUniverse books may be ordered through booksellers or by contacting:

iUniverse
1663 Liberty Drive
Bloomington, IN 47403
www.iuniverse.com
1-800-Authors (1-800-288-4677)

ISBN: 978-1-4620-0820-9 (sc)
ISBN: 978-1-4620-0821-6 (hc)
ISBN: 978-1-4620-0819-3 (ebk)

Printed in the United States of America

iUniverse rev. date: 11/17/2011

# Acknowledgements

I must acknowledge and thank some of the people who have inspired and helped in the creation of this little book. Doctor Pam Williams for answers to some complex medical questions; Doctor 'Bud' Miller for astutely critiquing early and final drafts; fellow members of the Idaho Writers' League, especially Gary Townsend, who offered constructive criticism at our chapter meetings; and last, but certainly not least, my wife, Pam, without whose constant support and encouragement this little book would have never happened.

This story is a work of fiction. But as is the case with most fiction, there are kernels of truth buried within it. The characters, names, incidents and dialog are products of the author's imagination and are not to be construed as real. That said, I must also thank those few individuals with whom I had the honor and privilege of working years ago in another, very different life. Be assured you are protected now, even as we were then. Cheers.

# Chapter 1

Monday, 6:40 p.m.

Karin was staggering now, and it was all Reed could do to hold her up and keep her moving across the restaurant parking lot to his car. He shoved her against the side of his Mercedes and held her there with one arm while fumbling with the door, finally getting it open, and dumping her into the front passenger seat. Once inside, she collapsed against the backrest.

He leaned into the car and tried to fasten her seat belt as she struggled to speak. Her words were slurred and nearly unintelligible. Then, for a moment, her speech became clearer, and he heard her say, "What's wrong with me? I need to go home. Call Deke." The seat belt snapped into place, and he quickly went around to the driver's side and slid behind the wheel. He started the car, and looking at Karin Jansen again, he thought, *You'll never go home again, and I am truly sorry for that. I really do like you, and I wish you had been willing to play when I asked you that time. But now all that is over.* She rolled toward the door and tried to speak again. But now Karin could neither move nor speak, and she slowly fell into a deep sleep, a coma from which she might never awaken.

———

Only an hour before, Tom Reed was standing on the steps of Karin Jansen's apartment building, trying to get his nerve up and wondering if he really could do what Robert Chilton had insisted that he must do.

Earlier in the day, Chilton had been adamant: "You've got to stop her." The two men were sitting in the front seat of Chilton's Cadillac in the deserted gravel parking lot in the rear of RFK Stadium. He continued,

Brian Cornett

"I can call in some favors and try to sidetrack the investigation of the senator's finances, but if she gets a deposition from those idiots in San Antonio, there's no way I can do anything. It's up to you to keep her from going to Texas tonight." He paused for a few seconds and then continued, "And then we'll make her disappear—permanently."

Reed looked hard at Senator Whiting's chief of staff. "Why me? I didn't have anything to do with his campaign." He wondered again what he had gotten himself into. Chilton had not seemed as ruthless and cold when they had first talked of stalling the attorney general's investigation into Whiting's finances. Reed looked away at the huge stadium for a moment and then turned back again to face Chilton. "You're the one who is covering up the contribution. All I did was introduce you to those people from Penta Systems." He stopped for a moment and then asked, "Do we have to go that far? Can't you think of another way? Maybe you could buy her off." He tried to think of some other, less drastic way to divert Karin from the investigation.

The older man looked at him and spoke softly, "Reed, you've told me that you want to move up in Washington politics, and for that you need my help. When we got you that job with the AG, you knew that we would want you to do some things that you might not want to do. Or are you turning ethical at last?" Chilton looked away and then spoke again, "It's a little late for that, so now you will do exactly as I say. You know I can make you in this town." He paused. "Or I can break you. If you don't take care of that nosy bitch from your office, I'll see that you are finished—forever." He turned away and looked through the windshield at the bright and sunny early fall day. "I think I know a way that you can keep her from leaving tonight."

Reed shifted uncomfortably in the plush seat of the car. "I don't know how you think we can stop her. She and I have a meeting with Garland to talk about the Penta deposition at ten this morning, and then I think she's taking the rest of the day off." He shrugged. "To go shopping, I suppose. Like most women." He turned to Chilton. "What are you thinking? Not kidnapping, I hope."

"Yes, actually, that's exactly what I have in mind. And I know just how you are going to be able to do it."

Karin Jansen was nearly finished packing for her working session in San Antonio and her vacation with Deke Mitchell in Port Mansfield when the doorbell of her Georgetown apartment sounded.

"Yes. Who's there?" she spoke into the intercom.

"It's Tom Reed, Karin. Can I come up?"

She wondered why one of the lawyers she worked with had come at five in the afternoon. "Sure, Tom. I'll buzz you in." She'd been with him in a conference at the office until noon and then left to have lunch with Deke before coming home to pack for the trip.

She opened the door when he knocked. Tom Reed stood there with a bouquet of roses in one hand and a bottle of Chardonnay in the other. *What's this?* She thought as she eyed the flowers and wine. *What is he up to? He knows I'm leaving tonight, and I've made it clear that I will never go out with him.*

"What's up, Tom? Not a crisis, I hope. My flight from Reagan National leaves at eight, you know."

Tom held out the flowers and the wine. "No, no problems. I just want to wish you a good trip and a great vacation." He smiled as she took the flowers.

"Thank you, Tom." She turned away, wondering why the sudden cordiality. She and Tom Reed had both worked for the United States attorney general for almost three years and had only socialized on a handful of occasions. Karin knew that Tom had been in a successful and lucrative private practice in Philadelphia before he joined the attorney general's staff. While they made good money in government service, she believed he lived well beyond his means. She knew that Reed, in his early forties and married to his third trophy wife, aspired to be a major player in the Washington social scene and had a reputation as a ladies' man. Of medium height, he spent time weekly with a personal trainer in an effort to create the image of an athlete. Many women found his dark, Irish good looks attractive, but Karin didn't. He was polished and could be charming both in and out of the courtroom, but she considered him to be trying too hard to be what he wasn't—a gentleman. They both worked in the civil case division of the AG's office. Early in their association, he had tried to romance her, but she had made it clear that their relationship would be strictly business, and since then, he had respected that position. Now they were both assigned to a case involving one of the senior members of the United States Senate. Although they had worked together on cases before

3

and she had gone on vacations and several short trips of three or four days, he had never given her flowers or wished her bon voyage in the past. Again, she wondered what he was really up to.

Karin turned back and held the bouquet out to him. "These flowers are lovely, Tom, but I may be gone for two weeks or more. Remember? They'll just be wasted here. Why don't you take them home to Susan? I'm sure she'll love to have them."

"God, you're right. What was I thinking?" He thrust the bottle of wine toward her. "Well, take this wine with you if you've got room to pack it. It's supposed to be a good vintage, and you can enjoy it while you're down there in Texas or wherever the hell you're going."

"I'm sure I have room for it. And thank you. We will enjoy it. I have a few more things to pack, and I can find a place to fit this in." Karin gestured toward the small wet bar nestled in the alcove between bookcases, which was filled with an eclectic collection of hardbound classics, law books, and current best sellers. "Tom, if you'd like a drink, there's Scotch and bourbon over there. Help yourself." She watched as Reed dropped the bouquet of roses on the coffee table and moved to the bar. He chose Scotch, the McCallan, and poured a double shot over a couple of ice cubes. "Could I make you a drink too?" His question came almost as an afterthought.

"No, thank you. Not now." She turned toward the bedroom and said, "I'll be here just a few more minutes."

Reed spoke quickly before she could enter the other room, "Would you like to have a quick dinner somewhere, Karin? You know they don't feed you on these evening flights anymore. I could take you to Reagan afterwards. Save you the parking fee." Tom sipped at his Scotch while he waited for her answer.

"I was going to take a cab." She paused. "But that would work for me as long as I get to the airport in time to get through the security stuff. It's a hassle sometimes, but I'm all right with it, and Deke says it helps. But it's hard to be sure that it has any real effect."

"Swell." Tom took another swallow of his drink. "Where would you like to eat? How about somewhere here in Georgetown?"

"That would be fine. If you can handle Italian, how about Polo's on Wisconsin? It's close, and the food and service are excellent. They shouldn't have much of a crowd this early, so we could be in and out in plenty of time. I'll be finished in here in just a few more minutes. Honest." She moved into her bedroom. "Make yourself comfortable."

———

Drink in hand, Reed moved restlessly around the living room. His offer to make her a drink had failed. Now he had to come up with another way to administer the drug Chilton had given him. He moved toward the window and looked down on the street. The last time he had been in her apartment was a year or so earlier, when Karin hosted a small cocktail party. He remembered that it was a two-bedroom, two-bath place with a large kitchen fully outfitted for a gourmet chef. He wondered now if she really was that good a cook and then decided that she probably was. She seemed to excel at anything she put her mind to. He was chuckling over a collection of framed *New Yorker* cartoons that were arranged on the wall opposite the little bar when he heard the buzz of her cell phone.

The phone, set to vibrate, was lying on the coffee table. Reed looked toward the bedroom doorway, realized that she had not heard the buzz, and quickly picked it up. He saw that the call was from David Mitchell, her boyfriend. He glanced at the doorway again, smiled slightly, and switched the phone to answer and then to disconnect without speaking. He dropped it back on the coffee table and slid it under the bouquet of flowers.

"I guess that's it." Karin came back into the room. "If you're finished with your drink, we'd better go."

"Sure. Let me help you with your bags." Reed went back to the bar and put his nearly empty glass in the sink before he picked up the suitcase she had brought from the bedroom. He hefted it a couple of times, making a show of being surprised at the weight. "Hey, what's in this thing? You taking all your law books to Texas?"

Karin picked up her purse and laptop case and slung the straps over her shoulder. "No law books, but I do have some files to review before I meet with those people at Penta Systems in San Antonio. As Garland told us this morning, they're probably going to be subpoenaed in the Senator Whiting campaign fund case. I think the three of us are supposed to meet with the senator when I get back from vacation. I want to talk to these people in San Antonio first." Karin paused and looked at her coworker. "What do you think of those rumors that Whiting found some other source of campaign funds that he didn't disclose? The Penta folks seem to be pretty upset about being suspected of not declaring all of their contribution to his campaign."

Reed frowned. "I don't know what to think about the rumors." He shrugged. "But after all, they are just rumors. I can't figure out why the AG is so concerned about the whole deal." He started toward the apartment door. "What are you and what's-his-name going to do in Texas? Didn't you tell Garland that his place is down on the coast somewhere?"

Karin laughed. "Deke has a house and a boat down there, and I guess he'll want to spend some time fishing in the Gulf. I'll just go along for the ride while he tries to catch dinner for us every day. There are some books in that suitcase, so I'll have something to read while he does his thing."

They were on the stairway leading to the street when Reed asked, "But don't you fish? I thought all of you people from Michigan were fishermen." They exited the building and headed for his car, which was parked illegally at the curb.

"No. Dad teaches at Michigan Tech in Houghton, but he isn't much of an outdoorsman, so we didn't learn to do all that. We spent our time skiing and skating." She laughed. "Deke has promised to teach me to fish, and we tried it the last time we were in the Florida Keys, but the weather turned bad, so I didn't get much practice. Maybe the Gulf will be different off the Texas coast."

Reed shrugged. "I wasn't much for the great outdoors either. Had to work too hard for the grades to get into Harvard." He opened the trunk of his new white Mercedes and shoved Karin's bag in while she settled into the soft leather of the passenger seat. The car was a four-door luxury power statement, all tan leather and real wood trim, fully equipped with all the bells and whistles.

Reed slid into the driver's seat. "Okay, Polo's it is." The big Mercedes purred its way through the early evening traffic of Georgetown, and in less than fifteen minutes, they pulled into the small parking lot beside the restaurant on Wisconsin Avenue. He came around to open her door, but Karin had already stepped out of the car and was headed for Polo's canopied entrance. He followed a pace or two behind, admiring her trim figure and wishing he didn't have to do what he intended.

Carlo, the maître d', welcomed Karin with a smile. "Good evening, Miss Jansen. Good to see you again. How have you been? Right this way." Never giving her a chance to answer, he scooped two menus from the rack and led them to a table, barely glancing at Reed. He pulled the chair out for Karin and opened her napkin, spreading it across her lap when she was seated. "A cocktail or wine this evening?"

Reed answered quickly, "Wine, I think." He turned to Karin. "Chianti all right with you?"

She nodded, and he turned back to Carlo. "A bottle of Ruffino. Miss Jansen has to catch a plane, so hurry it up." *This jerk doesn't know who I am,* Reed thought. *But he damn sure will the next time I come into this place.* He pulled out his chair and sat down.

"Of course. Your server will be right with you." Carlo smiled at Karin and turned away.

After their server brought the wine and they ordered, Karin settled back and turned to Reed. "Let's talk about the Senator Whiting case for a minute. You're pretty close to some guy on his staff, aren't you?"

Reed picked up his wine, took a small sip, and smiled. "Karin, I know a lot of the staffers up on the hill. I think I've played cards or golf with most of the important ones, but I don't remember anyone from Whiting's office in particular." Reed sipped his wine and watched Karin's face, trying to see if she believed him. He wondered if she knew of his relationship with Robert Chilton, the senator's chief of staff. Whiting was a very powerful senior member of the Senate, and Tom Reed had made it a point to get to know Chilton. They socialized frequently and had developed a mutually beneficial working relationship. In fact, it had been Chilton and Whiting who had arranged for him to join the attorney general's staff.

He really didn't want to discuss the Whiting case with her. He knew that the rumors were true. Robert Chilton had found another source of campaign funds for the senator, and because it was apparently a great deal of money coming from a foreign source, the chief of staff had thought it best to keep it hidden. Now it appeared that the cover-up might be discovered. The AG's office had received information concerning the funds, and an unofficial preliminary investigation had been opened. Penta Systems, an electronics importer in San Antonio, had donated to the senator's campaign, and the amount had been disclosed properly, but under the Campaign Finance Act, they were going to be questioned about the rumors of the hidden contributions. Reed decided to offer an innocuous comment: "Well, the people in San Antonio may know something, but I really doubt it."

"I don't know what they'll be able to tell me, but maybe there's some fire under all the smoke." Karin picked up her purse and rummaged through it. "Excuse me for a moment, Tom. I want to call Deke." She looked up. "Damn, I must have left my cell phone at the apartment. We'll have to swing by there again on our way to the airport and get it. Seems like we're all lost without those things." She hesitated. "Tom, I think you left that bouquet there too."

"Yes, I guess I did. We can get that stuff on the way to the airport." He pointed to the rear of the restaurant. "Maybe there's a phone back there at the bar that you can use."

Karin stood up and, before he could react and leave his seat, moved off toward the rear of the restaurant and the bar where the phones were located. He settled back down and slipped his hand into his jacket pocket. He fingered the small plastic vial of GHB. He had hoped to be able to slip some of it into Karin's drink at her apartment, but her refusal of the offer of a drink had left him wondering how he would be able to do it. Now was his best chance. He had no intention of using the date-rape drug in the usual manner. He only wanted to make her ill and eventually unconscious as he and Robert had planned. What happened after that was not up to him; Chilton had told him he would take care of that part.

As soon as she was safely away from the table, Reed pulled the vial of GHB from his pocket, uncapped it, and poured half of the colorless, tasteless liquid into Karin's nearly full glass of Chianti and then emptied the other half into her water glass. He didn't know what dosage would produce the effect he wanted. He had never had to resort to a drug like this. The vial held a little over an ounce, and he emptied it, knowing that he didn't have a lot of time and wanting it to work before she left on her flight. Robert Chilton had not told him how much to use.

Karin came back to the table, and he stood up. "Did you reach him all right?" Reed watched as she picked up her glass and took a swallow of the doctored wine, making a face at the taste of the Chianti.

"No, he didn't answer. I think he may still be at work, and he sometimes can't take calls there." She sipped her wine again. "The first taste of Chianti always surprises me. This one seems a little raw, don't you think?"

"Should have ordered a Reserva, I guess. That's usually a little smoother. But this isn't too bad." He took a long drink and refilled both of their glasses. "Gets better as you drink more of it, doesn't it?"

The server placed their orders on the table and asked the usual questions, received the usual replies, and withdrew. The restaurant was beginning to fill with early diners, and the noise level increased noticeably as they began to eat. Ten minutes into the meal, Reed was startled when Karin's fork clattered against her plate as it slipped from her fingers. Reed watched her carefully. He had no idea of how long it would take for the drug to work. Karin slumped back in her chair and shook her head, as if trying to clear a sudden fog. "Are you all right?" His tone was solicitous, and he reached over and gripped her arm to steady her.

"I don't know. All of a sudden I don't feel very well." Karin's speech was slurred as if she had drunk far more than part of one glass of wine.

"Maybe we should get out of here and get some fresh air." He pushed her water glass toward her. "You'd better drink your water. That might help."

Karin nodded and reached for the water glass, nearly spilling it as she tried to pick it up. Reed held his breath, hoping she wouldn't waste the last of the GHB. Finally, by using both hands, she brought it to her mouth and gulped down most of the contents.

She braced herself on the table and rose unsteadily. "Yes, we'd better get outside. I'm beginning to feel nauseous, and I don't want to be sick in here." Reed took her arm with one hand and dropped a fifty and a twenty on the table with the other.

"That should cover it. Let's go." He put his arm around Karin's waist, shoved her purse under her arm, and steered her toward the door. Nodding to Carlo as they passed his station, he said, "Miss Jansen isn't feeling well. I'll take care of her. I'm sure she'll be fine." Carlo stared at him as he pushed Karin through the door and guided her across the parking lot to his car.

# Chapter 2

Deke opened and closed the top drawer of his seldom-used desk for at least the tenth time. The drawer was empty. He'd already emptied it and the other three drawers and placed their meager contents in the small cardboard box resting on the government-issue, gray desktop. His cubicle was empty of anything that might be called personal. All the cubicles in the RECOM office were the same. No personal items were to be found in any of them. There were no pictures on the desks or clippings on the walls. The transients in the world of RECOM didn't carry much personal baggage, at least not the kind that could be put in a desk drawer or hung on a cube wall.

RECOM was listed in the yellow pages of the local directory under "Advertising Sales," but no one working there ever sold advertising. Deke's own business card read "David K. Mitchell, Account Executive" and listed a telephone number that, when called, was answered by an anonymous voice in a big, gray building in Langley, Virginia. The RECOM office itself was one of a dozen storefronts in a small strip mall in Chantilly, Virginia, well outside the beltway surrounding the nation's capital. It contained six open cubicles and one private office but no computers and no telephones. Secure cell phones and even more secure laptops were the rule. The blinds covering the windows were never opened, and a boldly lettered CLOSED sign was posted on the door over the telephone number. The cubicles were occupied only sporadically by the half-dozen agents assigned to RECOM. RECOM itself was a sham, an acronym without words to back it up.

And so were the people who sometimes occupied the cubes and drifted in and out of that small office. They were not who or what they appeared to be. Deke knew what he had been for the past twenty-five years. Now at forty-seven, he was retiring from the Company and RECOM to see if he could find out who he really was. He was quitting while he was still healthy. At six feet two and 193 pounds, he sported a few gray hairs and a number of scars but was in good condition otherwise. He passed the mandatory physical fitness tests required by the Company every six months without any problem. He worked out regularly to ensure that. He had been a standout athlete in high school and college, and he prided himself on staying in shape. One of the chief reasons RECOM and its parent considered him such a valuable asset was his good physical and mental condition, but they had also invested a great deal of time and money to ensure that he was well trained in the skills that a black operations unit like RECOM required. But now he was tired and wanted to move on.

Five days away from retirement, all that remained for him to do was to be debriefed by his boss, Jack Frazier, complete a mound of paperwork, and visit the CIA headquarters at Langley for his final out-briefing and farewell handshake from the director. There would be no farewell party. There never were farewell parties for the retirees or the others who sometimes disappeared. They were seldom mentioned and quickly forgotten. The faceless bureaucrats in the upper echelons at Langley stayed as far removed from RECOM's small group of specialists as they could. RECOM's budget, buried deep in the black area of the annual requests for money that Congress approved, had never been disclosed to any oversight committee. RECOM's people were not the sort that Washington's high and mighty were likely to socialize with, or even acknowledge, except on very rare occasions.

Deke pushed his chair back and got up from the desk. Picking up the small box, he stepped into the narrow passageway separating the cubes and turned toward Jack Frazier's office. Pete Sanders unfolded his six-foot-five-inch frame from his gray office chair and spoke as Deke passed his open cube, "Ready to call it quits, Deke? Or are you going to hang around till Saturday?" Pete was one of the very few who called him by his nickname, a corruption of his first two initials.

"Just about finished, Pete. Have to see the boss and get my brain scrubbed clean and then go back out to Langley tomorrow. Will probably spend most of the day out there finishing up the paperwork. Then I'm going to take a couple days of terminal leave, so I can get out of here." He and Pete had worked together on several assignments since the big man joined RECOM four years earlier, and they often stopped at one of the local pubs for a drink or two after work when both happened to be in town. "Flying to Texas on Thursday morning. And then it's a couple of weeks of fishing in the Gulf."

"Got time for a brew later?" Pete came out of his cube and extended his hand. "Or are you going to meet Karin?"

Deke glanced at his watch before he shook the proffered hand. "Yes to the brew, and no, I'm not meeting her. We had lunch together today and she's leaving for San Antonio this evening. She has some meetings scheduled there for tomorrow and the next day. I'll meet her when she's through, and we'll drive on down to Port Mansfield." He paused. "How about I meet you at Ruby Tuesday when Jack gets through with me? We'll probably be through around six."

"Sounds good. I'll grab us a table." Sanders turned back into his cube, and Deke stepped to the closed door of Jack Frazier's office and knocked twice before entering.

He dropped the box on the corner of his boss's desk. "Okay, Jack. I'm about to get out of here. You ready to brainwash me? Take all those nasty secrets out of my head in one fell swoop?" Deke and Jack both knew that the debriefing was merely a formality. A signature on a piece of paper could never erase everything that a man had learned or been a party to in twenty-five years of working for the CIA. That piece of paper merely ensured that those who signed could never talk about any of it.

Frazier reached into the bottom drawer of his desk and hauled out a bottle of Jim Beam and two glasses. "Pull up a chair, Deke. We need to talk for a little bit." He leaned forward in his motorized wheelchair and poured an inch of bourbon in a glass for Deke and two inches into his own. "How are you and Karin doing? Ready to tie the knot?"

"Not real sure about that." Deke took a sip of the bourbon. "Karin isn't either. That's why we're going to Texas for a couple of weeks. To get it all figured out. We had a long discussion about that at lunch today." He took another small sip. "I've been through the marriage thing once before, you know."

"Yeah. I remember Barbara. She still in Seattle?"

"I guess so. I don't hear from her very often." Deke's face brightened. "Got a short note from Jeff last week. Says he may start a couple of games for the Huskies this season. Likes playing linebacker, and he had good spring and preseason practices."

"Man, time flies. How old is he now?"

"Turned twenty last May. He's a junior this year. I'm going to go up there to see him play after Karin and I get back from Texas." He watched as Jack poured another two inches of bourbon for himself. Deke hated to see him drink like that, but ever since Jack had been confined to that chair, he had been drinking heavily. Deke knew it was his way of dulling the pain that never quite went away. Jack could have taken disability retirement after the two of them had nearly been killed in Beirut in '97 but elected to stay on to become the chief of RECOM. He had taken the job in July of 2001 after his recovery and rehab. Deke guessed that he had opted for desk duty because he had nothing else to go to.

And Deke? What did he have? A little money in the bank, a decent boat, and a small house in Port Mansfield on the Texas Gulf Coast. An ex-wife living in Seattle whom he seldom heard from and a son in college whom he saw rarely. He and Barbara had divorced when the boy was seven, and she had moved to Seattle. Deke had missed his son's growing-up years, and he deeply regretted that. He also had a sometime girlfriend whom he almost believed he loved. In the next two weeks, they hoped to learn more about whether or not they loved each other enough to marry. Now he was facing his boss across the desk and hearing him say, "Been a slight change of plans, Deke." Jack was another of those who called him by his nickname. The deep, livid scar across Jack's face caused his grin to be lopsided, but there was a glint of humor in his eye. "You're going to have to keep your brain dirty for a little while longer."

"What are you talking about? I'm retired as of midnight Friday night."

"Well, that's not exactly true anymore. You've got just one more little job. Shouldn't take you more than a week, ten days at the most." He hesitated and then continued, "I really hate to do this to you, Deke, but you know the Middle East better than anyone else we've got. I only got the go-ahead on this from Langley about twenty minutes ago, or I would have told you about it sooner. You're booked on a flight to Pakistan out of Dulles in the morning. I'll pick you up at your place at five and take you out there. We might have some additional information by then, and I can brief you on the way, but if not, Jamie Wilson will meet you in Karachi and bring you up to speed."

"Aw, for Christ's sake, Jack. You're really screwing me up with this." Deke put his hands palm down on the desk and leaned toward his boss. "I'm scheduled to be out-briefed at Langley tomorrow, and then I'm taking a couple of days of terminal leave. I'm retiring, Jack. Remember? I've already booked a flight to Texas for Thursday morning, and Karin's leaving tonight for San Antonio." He took a deep breath and said, "Jack, there had better be a damn good reason why I need to be doing this."

"There really is a damn good reason why I have to give you this job." He moved his motorized wheelchair out from behind the desk. "Cliff Scott and twenty million dollars have gone missing in Pakistan. The money was couriered in via diplomatic pouch, and Cliff signed for it. Now we don't know what happened to him, and we've got to find out and recover that money before it gets into the wrong hands. Langley Ops thinks part of it is earmarked for terrorist operations here in the States. Maybe all of it. They're calling this Operation Swift Mission, and it is really high priority with a short timetable. Langley Ops wants it wrapped up in less than a week if you can do it."

Deke sat back down. "I haven't been in Pakistan in three, no, four years. Now with all the stuff going on in Afghanistan, I'm sure a lot of things have changed. Is Jamie on top of things?"

"Sure. But he's not part of RECOM, just the deputy station chief over there. He can't do anything but gather intel and report. That's why we need you to go. You're the best and most experienced field man we've got."

"All right. Let me call Karin and let her know I won't be meeting her in San Antonio." He hit her speed-dial number on his cell phone. After three rings, her phone went dead. He stared at it for a minute and then put it back in his pocket.

"No luck?"

Jack's question brought him back. "Don't know what's wrong. Must be a problem on her end. She could be on her way to the airport, I guess. I'll try her again later." He leaned over the desk. "You'd better be right about this only taking a few days, Jack, 'cause I'm through as soon as I get back." He swallowed the last of the whiskey in his glass and picked up the small cardboard box again. "I'll see you in the morning."

He had turned and started for the door when Frazier spoke again. "You'd better pack wet. You never know how things are going to be over there."

# Chapter 3

"Where is she?" Robert Chilton dropped into the leather chair opposite Tom Reed in the main lounge of the Watergate. The place was rapidly filling up with the usual lunch crowd. The tables near the overloaded buffet were occupied by the powerful and near-powerful players of the Washington political scene. Chilton kept his voice low even though they were sitting at a small table far enough removed from most of the crowd to avoid being overheard. "You said you would put her in a safe place. What did you do with her?"

Reed took a long drink from his glass of Scotch. Even for him, it was early in the day to be drinking, but he really needed this one. He glanced around before he answered the older man's question. "She's up at that old hunting camp off Route 29 northeast of Romney. You've been up there, I think. It might have been years ago when it was a shooting range. I didn't want to put her in a motel here in the city, and she'll be safe up there until you decide what to do." Reed was tired. He had driven Karin Jansen to the camp the night before and stayed most of the night with her. She passed out in the car from the dose of GHB he had given her, and never awakened. He figured she'd stay out for a day or so. The hunting camp was a prime piece of real estate on the South Fork of the Potomac River. It had once been a private gun club used by members of Congress and a select group of the Washington elite who partied in the main lodge building and challenged each other on the two-hundred-yard shooting range. While it had been closed for several years, access was still available to a chosen few, but hardly anyone used it anymore, especially at this time of the year. Reed figured it would be a good place to hide Karin until

Chilton could arrange for her disappearance or whatever he had in mind. "She was still unconscious when I left her early this morning."

"For Christ's sake, how much of that stuff did you give her?"

Reed grimaced. "All of it." He took a quick drink of his Scotch. "You didn't tell me how much to use."

Chilton leaned forward. "You might have killed her with that much."

"Well, if I did, it's your fault. I never used that stuff before."

"It really doesn't matter. I'll see that she is taken care of. Is she locked up, or can she get away? You did tie her up, didn't you?"

"No. She was really out, and I think she'll stay that way for a while."

Chilton turned on him. "You goddamn idiot. You're not supposed to think. She could come to any time. I know that place is pretty remote, but we don't want her wandering around." He paused. "But maybe that wouldn't be a bad way for her to disappear at that. Lost in the woods." He smiled a little. "I'll have to think about that."

Reed picked up his glass again. "I locked her in one of the bedrooms in the old lodge building. I put some bottled water in the room with her in case she does wake up. I'll go back up there to check on her, maybe tomorrow." He stopped. "Unless that won't be necessary."

"No. You'll get your ass back up there today and tie her up or chain her to the bed or something. I don't care what you do. Just make damn sure she stays put. I can't do anything about her until early next week. You'll have to keep track of her until then." Chilton waited until a passing waiter had moved out of range. "I'll let the senator know that we have things under control. At least she won't be at the meeting in San Antonio this morning. I'm afraid those people at Penta Systems will give up too much information if the AG's office starts to put pressure on them. After all, they're the ones who introduced me to those other ragheads and got us involved with them and their promises, and they'll want to cover their asses. The senator should never have accepted the offer of that money, but it's hard to resist a five-million-dollar contribution. Now I've just found out that it might be coming from the Middle East." He smiled at the younger man. "But I'm sure we can manage to keep Penta Systems happy and quiet. I know they're hungry for business, and defense contracts are always good."

Reed finished his drink and signaled the waiter that he wanted another. "All right. I'll go back up there and take care of her if I can get away from the office this afternoon. If I can't, I'll go first thing in the morning. I'll call you later and let you know her condition."

"Don't be an idiot, Reed." Chilton's voice was sharp. "No phone calls. With all the stuff that's going on about eavesdropping and wiretaps, even cell phones might not be safe. I don't want the NSA calling on me—or you. Meet me here again tomorrow, same time. I'll see the senator in the morning before his early committee meeting. You just take care of that woman. That's your job." He dropped a ten-dollar bill on the low table and stood up. "Are you sure she won't be missed for a few days?"

"No. Garland knows she's going on vacation after the meeting today." Reed smiled. "And I told him she had called me this morning to let me know she's gotten to San Antonio all right."

"Good. That's the smartest thing you've done so far. Go on back to work. I'm sure you can find something constructive to do. If you can, find out how much Garland really knows."

Reed watched the big man go through the room. Chilton spoke to some of the men and women, waved a greeting to a few, and deliberately ignored others. Robert Chilton was a very powerful man. A former lobbyist, now he was Senator Whiting's right-hand man and principal adviser, and the senator was the chairman or senior member of several important committees. Tom Reed hoped to have a job like that someday, and Robert Chilton had promised to help him get it. That's why Tom had given up his law practice in Philadelphia and taken the job with the AG. Chilton and the senator had helped him get it with the understanding that he would keep them informed about things the AG's office was involved in. Tom knew that if they could quash this inquiry into the senator's finances, he would be one giant step closer to moving up, and while he was worried about what he was doing and what would happen to Karin, he believed the end justified the means. He knew that, as far as Chilton believed, the kidnapping and ultimate disappearance of Karin Jansen was crucial, and the man had no qualms about what would happen to her.

# Chapter 4

Pete Sanders appeared to be having a problem with the large cardboard box he carried as he followed the elderly woman up the steps of Karin's apartment building. He smiled at the woman and asked, "Could you hold the door for me, please, ma'am?" The box he was carrying insured that she would comply. The box was empty. There were twelve apartments in the building, four on each floor. Karin's was on the second floor, and Pete quickly found her door. He donned two pair of latex surgical gloves, picked the flimsy class B door lock, and entered the apartment.

Pete moved carefully around the living room. Everything seemed to be in order except for a wilting bouquet of roses lying on the coffee table. When he got to the little bar, he saw a glass in the sink with perhaps a half inch of water in it. Spreading his fingers on the inside of the glass, he picked it up and looked at it closely. There were smudges on the outside which he thought were fingerprints. He sniffed the glass, decided it had contained Scotch, poured out the water, and carefully put the glass into a plastic bag.

Nothing seemed out of the ordinary in either of the bedrooms, the kitchen, or the bathroom. Karin's cosmetics were not in evidence, nor could he find any luggage or her laptop. Returning to the living room, a quick look around assured him that he left no trace. He recovered the empty box and left, locking the door again. Stripping off the gloves in the hall, he stuffed them in his jacket pocket and made his way downstairs. He'd dispose of the gloves when he got back to the RECOM office. Outside again, he dropped the box into the bed of his pickup and walked around the building. Karin's car was in the carport space allotted to her. He made certain that it was locked, and headed for his truck.

Jack Frazier looked up when Pete knocked and came into his office. "Any problem, Pete?"

"No, boss. Got in and out without anyone noticing what I was doing. Found a drinking glass that may have some prints. I'll run it out to the lab at the Farm and see what they can find. Probably won't have anything definite until tomorrow or Friday. She evidently left as scheduled. No luggage around, and her laptop isn't there."

"No. Use the FBI lab downtown since this is unofficial and concerns one of us. I don't want the people at Langley involved. Besides, the FBI lab will probably be faster. Then go check the flights to San Antonio that left Monday night. Deke said she was supposed to leave from Reagan around eight, I think. See if she was on any of the passenger lists. She may not have gotten out of here as scheduled. If she's in Texas, I'll have to call someone down there."

Pete laughed. "Hell, Jack, I'll be happy to go to San Antone and look for her. I was stationed down there for a while when I was in the air force. It's a great city."

Jack grinned his lopsided grin. "No. You don't get a vacation on my dime. I've got some other things for you to do here. And, depending on what Deke finds, I may have to send you to help him. So stay loose. Right now, get on the airport thing. Let's be sure Karin left Washington. And get moving on this, Pete. Deke's got his hands full over there, but he's afraid something is seriously wrong." Jack dismissed him with a wave, and Pete went to his cube and retrieved the glass.

A little over an hour later, he walked into the crime lab in the FBI building in downtown Washington. He showed his credentials to the guard at the door and was admitted to the lab's outer office. The RECOM agents often worked with their counterparts in the other national and state-level intelligence and law enforcement agencies. There were five technicians in the lab, but Pete chose to hand the glass to the short, dark-haired, and very pretty Asian-American technician on duty. He told her what he wanted. She smiled and promised to get to it as soon as she had finished her current task.

Pete smiled at the pretty young woman. "If you can do it before lunch, I'll buy."

The girl smiled back and said, "Thanks anyway. But it'll be late this afternoon before I can get to it."

"That's fine. How about dinner then? And I'm still buying." Pete hoped she'd accept. "What can I call you? And what time should I come back?"

"You can call me Angela. Around five o'clock will be fine. I may have something for you by then." She tilted her head and said, "What did you have in mind for dinner? I'm not overly particular. Most anything will suit me."

"How about tapas? I know a great new place not far from here. They have great mojitos and sangria, and the food's good too." He smiled at her again as she nodded her approval. "I'll be back at five, if that's all right."

At Reagan National Airport, Pete showed his credentials to the manager and told him that he needed to see the passenger manifests for the San Antonio-bound flights of the previous Monday. The central computer quickly confirmed that Karin Jansen had been a no-show for American Airlines flight 543.

"Could you check the manifests out at Dulles for me?" Pete asked the manager.

"Sure. Our computers are linked. San Antonio flights only?"

"Yeah. Let's see what turns up."

But nothing did. Checking her name against all San Antonio flights for Monday and Tuesday at both airports failed to turn up anything. Karin Jansen had not left the Washington area for San Antonio on Monday night or Tuesday, at least not by air.

# Chapter 5

Wednesday, 10:00 a.m.

Karachi looked the same as it had the last time he had passed through the crowded city. The ride into the heart of town from the airport was along the same hot, dusty, crowded boulevard, flanked on both sides with open-air stalls. Painted billboards towered over them and were perched on every building. Deke could never understand why the billboards in nearly all of the countries in the Middle East, touting the ubiquitous American soft drinks and automobiles, were painted rather than printed and pasted up. He guessed labor was cheaper than paper. The smells of burning charcoal, diesel exhaust, and roasting meat and spices spilled through the open windows of the taxi along with the dust stirred up by the donkeys, trucks, and occasional camels that they passed. The driver eventually forced his way through the pedicabs and bicycles and pulled up to the entrance of the Imperial Hotel, a seven-story high-rise that had seen better days. When it was new, in the sixties, the Imperial was a showplace, but it had not aged gracefully. The marble steps were beginning to crack and chip here and there, and the lawn, once covered with lush, well-watered grass, now showed bare spots and a litter of the dry, brown palm fronds which had fallen from the unwatered palms lining the driveway. When he pushed through the lobby doors, Deke found that the air-conditioning still worked. Cool air washed over him, and even though it had a faint musty odor, he welcomed the relief from the already sweltering Pakistani morning.

When he reached the desk and handed his passport to the clerk, the turbaned Pakistani flashed a toothy smile, pushed a registration card toward him and returned his passport. The building wasn't the only thing that had not aged well. Service and civility had also slipped a little. The clerk hit the call bell, and an elderly Pakistani bellman shuffled across the tiled lobby. Deke was carrying only one bag and could have easily handled it himself, but he turned it over. The old man looked as though he could use the tip. Taking the key from the desk clerk, the porter shuffled off toward the elevators, and Deke followed. He handed the man a ten-rupee note, told him to put the bag in the room, and turned toward the bar.

Jamie Wilson, the deputy station chief from Islamabad was supposed to meet Deke, but he wasn't in the lobby. Knowing Jamie, Deke reasoned that he would be in the bar even if it was not yet noon. It would be cooler in there, and Jamie liked his comfort and the occasional morning drink. He too was an old Company hand, and Deke had worked with him before and knew that the drinking was part of his persona and that it had never affected his performance. Deke pushed through the louvered swinging doors of the bar and took a quick look around the dim room. Overhead fans turned lazily to keep the air moving much as in the days before air conditioning. The bar was nearly deserted. Two well-dressed young women sat at a small table watching the sweat bead on their glasses of gin and tonic. They looked up when Deke came through the door, but dismissed him with one swift glance. He wasn't the one they were waiting for, but he smiled at them anyway.

Jamie was crouched on a stool at the corner of the polished mahogany bar. He was a thin and wiry man, five inches shorter than Deke and perched on the bar stool like a spider in the center of its web. He watched Deke in the mirror as he entered the bar and now waved a languid hand toward the stool on his left, not bothering to turn around. Deke straddled the stool and waited for the dark-skinned bartender to acknowledge him. When the man sauntered over, Deke ordered a vodka tonic. Jamie had a tall Scotch and water in front of him.

"Good trip?" Jamie still hadn't turned away from the mirror and now Deke saw why. Sitting in the corner, reading a newspaper, was a man he hadn't noticed when he entered. Jamie was watching the man's reflection in the mirror.

"The usual drag. It's still sixteen hours in the air with a three-hour wait at London Heathrow in the middle. I did manage to get a little sleep on the plane." Deke sipped his drink and nodded toward the newspaper reader's reflection. "That someone you know?"

"No. But I think he knows me. Hasn't turned a page of that newspaper since he sat down. Came in right after I did. Apparently not very well trained. It's tough to get good help these days, I guess." Jamie took a sip of his drink. "Anyway, we can't talk here. Too quiet. There's a restaurant up on the top floor that should be open in a few minutes. I can brief you there while we have lunch. I imagine it's been awhile since they fed you on the plane." He paused. "Did Jack fill you in on the problem."

"Some of it. He said you probably had some more current information and maybe some pictures for me. Seemed in a hurry to get me over here, but it still takes a full day. You have anything new that I can use?" Deke glanced at his watch. It was two in the morning in Washington and one o'clock in San Antonio. Too early to call either Jack or Karin. He'd tried to call her on his cell phone several times while he was delayed in London but hadn't been successful. He figured that she had gone to San Antonio without knowing that he was leaving the country or that he wouldn't be able to meet her as they had planned. He didn't know what hotel she had booked, so he could call only her cell phone. He tried again as soon as he had landed in Karachi, but as before, there was no answer.

Jamie turned to him and frowned. "Yeah, some new things have popped up. Let's wait until we get upstairs."

"I'll meet you in the restaurant. Need to wash up and make a phone call first." Deke finished his drink and slid off the bar stool. "You can buy this one. You still owe me from last time."

As he turned toward the door, the man at the table looked up from his newspaper and caught his eye. He nodded and bent over the paper again. Deke didn't know him but suspected that the newspaper reader knew who he and Jamie were. He fixed the man's face in his memory as he had been trained to do—broad forehead, slightly hooked nose, olive skin, no moustache, and deep creases on both sides of his mouth. Deke would recognize him if he saw him again, and he was certain that would happen.

The cell phones the Company provided didn't need to rely on towers and were great as long as the satellites stayed up. Deke's phone was working, but Karin's was either broken or out of service for some other reason. It was the middle of the night in San Antonio, if that's where she was, and she should have answered. It wasn't like her to just disappear. He and Karin had been dating off and on for nearly two years, and they had begun to consider a serious relationship in the past six months. She had agreed to come to Texas for a week or two to see if they could stand each other on a more permanent basis. Now she was gone somewhere, and Deke was worried. He decided to call Jack later and see if he had learned anything further. Right now he needed to check on his bag and wash the travel grime off. When he got to his room, he found the bag on the folding rack at the end of the bed. The thin strip of nearly invisible tape he had placed on the rear hinge area was unbroken and unwrinkled, so he knew the bag had not been opened. He washed up quickly and headed for the restaurant.

Jamie was seated at a table by the window overlooking the crowded boulevard seven stories below. The room was nearly empty, and no one was sitting near enough to their table to hear what they were saying. The two women from the bar had also migrated upstairs as had the newspaper reader. He sat alone near the door to the kitchen, a good move if one needed to get out of the room in a hurry. Deke thought that maybe he wasn't such an amateur after all. He began to believe that the man wanted them to spot him and suggested this to Jamie.

"I think you're right. But I don't know whose side he's on. Hell, he might even be your contact." Jamie sipped at his fresh Scotch and water. "You're supposed to meet with a guy named Faraz. I've never seen him. He's the one in the al-Qaeda cell who was going to receive the money, but he passed the word to us that it didn't happen. Now there's twenty million bucks floating around out there somewhere, and you need to find it."

"Was Cliff Scott supposed to deliver it to this Faraz?"

Jamie frowned and turned to look out the window. "Yeah, Faraz was supposed to give up someone who is working both sides of the street. A double or triple agent." He paused and then said, "Cliff's one of the good guys. I don't like to think that something bad might have happened to him."

Deke didn't want to think about that possibility either. He and Scott had worked together once in Turkey, and he liked the young man. Cliff was a lot like he and Jack had been when they were new in the Company.

Deke picked up his bottled water and was about to take a drink when two men came through the door of the restaurant. One pointed toward the kitchen door, and Deke turned just in time to see their newspaper-reading friend disappear through it. The bigger of the two newcomers headed that way, and the other went back through the entry doors.

"Well, would you look at that?" Jamie picked up his drink again. "I wonder whose side they're on."

# Chapter 6

Wednesday, 1:10 p.m.

Twenty minutes later they found out.

The two men came back into the restaurant and went over to the table occupied by the women who had been in the bar. Pointing to the kitchen door, the smaller man appeared to ask them some questions. Both of the women shook their heads and then handed their passports to the man. He looked at them and handed them back. After a couple of minutes, the two men looked over at Jamie and Deke and came over to their table.

"Excuse me, gentlemen. Did you see the man who ran into the kitchen?" The bigger of the two dropped a cheap leather folder on the table. Jamie picked it up, glanced at it, handed it to Deke, and leaned back in his chair.

"Didn't pay any attention to him. Why do you ask?"

Deke looked at the identification card in the folder. The man's card and the badge identified him as an agent of the Pakistani Inter-Services Intelligence agency, the local equivalent of the CIA. Apparently, the newspaper reader was something else.

"Who was he?" Deke asked as he dropped the folder back onto the table.

The smaller of the two agents, obviously the boss, turned to him. About five feet seven inches tall, the man couldn't have weighed half as much as his partner. Bad teeth and a scraggly moustache competed for attention in the pockmarked face of the thoroughly ugly little man. "We thought you might know. Did he not come up here with you?" He picked up the big man's credentials and handed them back to his partner without taking his eyes away from Deke.

"Oh, no." Jamie was quick. "He wasn't with us. Never saw him before. And if you find him, I suppose no one will ever see him again." He picked up his drink. "Now would you mind letting us finish our lunch?"

"Certainly, we won't bother you anymore. If we could just see your passports, please. You're Americans?" Deke was sure the man knew very well who and what they were. They handed over their passports, and the ugly little man took his time examining the various stamps and visas. When he was satisfied, he tossed them back on the table, nodded, and said, "Thank you, gentlemen. Have a pleasant stay in Pakistan." He and his big partner turned and walked away.

Deke waited until they were out of earshot, took a drink of his bottled water, and turned to Jamie. "Now what? The Paks know we're here. They certainly know who you are, and now they can put me with you. Does that complicate my job any further, or is it complicated enough?" He knew already that he would have trouble acting with any freedom during his stay.

Jamie leaned forward. "As I told you, you probably have got to go to Peshawar. That's where the money was supposed to go, and the al-Qaeda-Taliban cell we're looking for is operating up there. They are funneling money and weapons to the Taliban across the border in Afghanistan. A lot of it is coming in from Iran, but a bunch of it comes through here. We'd like to find their pipeline and the guy who runs it. This Faraz was supposed to have the information and was going to turn the man over to us. Cliff was to meet with him up there." He took a long sip of his drink. "If that guy they are chasing was Faraz, I suppose he will go back to Peshawar now that his cover might be blown down here." He took another sip from his drink and continued, "The station chief told me that there's a rumor going around that some of the missing money is headed to the States to finance some sort of operation there."

"Something like 9/11?"

"We don't know, but we don't think so. The rumors are vague, but there have been some indications that there's a new cell in the States, perhaps in Texas."

Deke sat back and considered what he knew and what he had to work with. Jamie gave him a recent picture of Cliff Scott. Deke thought perhaps he could find someone in Peshawar who might have seen the agent there. Cliff was a crucial figure in this. Deke hated to think that he had taken the money and run, but he hated even more the thought that something bad had happened to the young man. But he still had a few more questions for Jamie.

"How big a package is twenty million dollars, Jamie?" He envisioned a huge suitcase or box of some sort.

"About briefcase-sized. It's in bearer bonds of one hundred thousand dollars face value. That's only two hundred pieces of paper." Jamie grinned. "Anyone can cash them at any bank that has that much money, anywhere in the world."

"Well, that makes it simple," Deke laughed. "We just have to find the bank that cashed one of these things. The Company has resources to do that. So why am I out here beating the bushes?"

Jamie sipped at his drink. "We haven't heard that any of the bonds have surfaced, and I doubt that whoever has them would try to cash any of them here in Pakistan."

"Yeah, I guess you're right about that. If I were going to try that, I'd go to Switzerland or London maybe. It would be easy enough to get a couple of hundred pieces of paper out of here. Hell, you could mail them one at a time to a drop anywhere."

"That's why you have to find whoever took them, so we know what happened to them and where they are now. Twenty million dollars isn't a lot of money in the big scheme of things, but it's a bit untidy to have it just disappear. People ask questions, and when they don't get answers they like, they ask more questions, and pretty soon a lot of the Company's laundry is hanging out there in public. I'm pretty sure you don't want to be responsible for something like that," he said to Deke. "I know I sure as hell don't."

"All right, I'll grab a flight to Peshawar in the morning and see what I can find. Are there any of our old Pak friends still up there? Anyone left over from when the air force operated that installation west of the city?"

"That was a long time ago, but there are still one or two around. Ahmed Kahn, the bartender at the Somerset Hotel, is a Sikh who has worked with us for a long time. He's totally reliable, and he should be able to help you. We have some other people up there in the territories, but they're either in the hills or in deep cover, and I don't want to bring them out for this."

"Good." Deke finished his water and stood up. "I'm going to get some sleep. If I need anything from you, I'll contact you in Islamabad." Jamie was going back that evening. They shook hands, and Deke headed for the elevator that would take him down to his room. The two young women were waiting for it to come up from the lobby.

The tall brunette turned to him as he walked up. "You're American, aren't you?" Her smile was friendly, and her accent was English.

"Guilty as charged." Deke smiled back at her. She was attractive, tall for a woman, close to five feet eight, and with a fair figure. She had regular features, but her eyes were a cold sea-gray. He noted that she was wearing low-heeled moccasin-type shoes and an expensive light-gray tweed suit. "From your accent, I assume you're English." The two women didn't look like tourists, but he thought he'd give them the chance to make up their own stories. "Just visiting, or do you work here?"

"Just a brief visit before we go on to Australia, I'm afraid. And you are right; we are from England. London, actually. Have you ever been there?" The brunette paused. "We're teachers on holiday. I'm Elizabeth, and this is Patricia."

The other woman, a short, curly-haired blonde smiled. "Are you just visiting also?" She was a shorter, more buxom version of her companion. Deke noted appreciatively that she was slightly chest heavy, a fact partially hidden by the tan linen jacket she wore over her square-necked, white blouse. The matching knee-length skirt failed to conceal the curves of her hips and well-tanned legs. In contrast to her friend, her eyes were blue with a hint of purple. Their clothes belied the claim that they were teachers. Deke knew that teachers in England didn't make enough money to dress as smartly fashionable as these two.

Too much information too soon. Deke's instincts took over, and he decided to play with them a little. "I'm Dave Mitchell, and I work for a contractor doing some major airport construction here. Been here about three months and expect to stay about six more. It's not a bad place if you know where to go to have a little fun now and then." They could mull all that over at their leisure and tell MI5 or 6 whatever they wished. He was certain they belonged to one or the other of the British intelligence services. The Pak security guys had gone to them first in the restaurant, and Deke suspected that those guys knew every foreign operative in Karachi. He wondered what these women were doing in Karachi when most of the spooks in Pakistan operated out of Islamabad under embassy cover. Were they shadowing him or Jamie? And why? He did not want to get the Brits involved in his operation. He needed to work alone.

The elevator came, and he held the door as the women entered. "Which floor?" he asked. The brunette reached past him and pushed the button for the fifth floor. Deke pushed the button for the lobby, and the elevator began its creaking descent. He didn't believe they had seen him come in earlier and register, so he planned to carry the deception a little further and leave the hotel. The brunette spoke again, "We've not had much chance to see the city except from the tour bus. Could you recommend a good restaurant? In the few days we've been here, we've stayed pretty close to this hotel." That was an invitation if he ever heard one, but he wasn't about to go there.

"Well, there are some fine places on Old Kingdom Road. It's a short cab ride, and any one of them is probably better than what you've been getting upstairs. I already have an engagement for this evening, or I would be happy to escort you both." He smiled at the little blonde. "But that's not possible tonight." He thought she looked disappointed. He nodded good-bye to them as the elevator doors opened on the fifth floor. He rode on down to the lobby and made for the front door. Outside, he considered what to do. It was too hot to walk very far, so he hailed a cab and told the driver to take him to the Pakistan International Airlines ticket office. He decided to get his ticket for the next day's flight to Peshawar, and during the twenty or thirty minutes it would take him to arrange that, the two women would be out of the way and he could get up to his room.

Before the cab could pull away, the old Pakistani porter shoved his hand through the window and dropped a folded piece of paper. Deke picked it up as the cab took off.

The note was short: "Intercontinental Hotel bar. Eight o'clock. Faraz."

Deke aborted the trip to the airline office and told the driver to drive around the city for a while. The cabbie looked at him as if he were crazy and mumbled some words in Urdu which Deke barely understood, but from the amount of grumbling and the look on the man's face, he gathered that the man really didn't want to fight the afternoon traffic in the crowded city. Deke made him drive around downtown Karachi for thirty minutes and then return to the hotel. Once again in his room, Deke opened his bag and released the hidden catch to the false bottom. He had taken Jack's advice and packed wet. The .45 caliber Glock 21, its two 13-round magazines, and the holster fit snugly in the recesses carved in the shielded Styrofoam of the case. No airport security scan had ever penetrated the shielding. After a shower in the tepid water that trickled from the rusted fixture over the stained tub, Deke lay down and tried to get a couple of hours of sleep. He wasn't suffering from jet lag very badly since he'd been able to sleep on the flight from London. He awoke around six thirty and tried to call Karin again. When he had no success, he dialed Jack Frazier's number.

It was eight thirty in the morning in Washington so he knew his boss would be in the office. When Jack answered, Deke's first question was this: "What have you found out about Karin?"

"I put Pete on it right after you left, but we don't have anything firm yet. Are you sure she left Washington Monday night?"

"I don't know anything for sure. She was scheduled out of Reagan around eight Monday night. I tried to call her a couple of times, but her cell phone has been out of service or cut off. As I told you the other morning, Pete and I had a couple of beers at Ruby Tuesday before I went home. It's not like her to just drop out of sight like this, and I'm worried."

"Okay, we're checking to see if she made the flight. And if she didn't, we'll find her. Should have some information for you by the end of the day."

Deke felt a little better after the call. Even though he was relatively new, Pete Sanders was one of the best agents in the RECOM group, and he would be able to find Karin if she were to be found at all. Deke dressed for his meeting with Faraz. The Glock fit snugly in the concealed carry holster at his waist, and his light microfiber sport jacket concealed it completely. Deke hoped that he would have no need for the weapon, but he felt a little more comfortable now that it was close at hand.

# Chapter 7

Pete walked through the door of the FBI lab at precisely five o'clock. Angela looked up from her desk and smiled. "You're right on time. Are you hungry or just eager to find out what was on the glass?"

"Both. Were you able to recover a usable print?"

"As a matter of fact, there were several good ones, two different sets, one new and one somewhat older. There's a really good left thumb and three fingers on the glass. They're the recent ones, and they belong to an attorney named Thomas Reed." The girl paused. "He's in the system because of his background check."

Angela moved some papers from the desktop to an out-basket. "The other set of prints on the glass also belong to an attorney—Karin Jansen. They were the older set." She stood up.

Pete smiled down at the girl who was barely five feet two. "The glass came from Karin's apartment." He picked up the plastic bag containing the glass and pocketed it. "I'd tell you more if I could." He took Angela's coat from the rack and held it as she slipped into it. "I really appreciate what you've done today. It'll be a big help."

"You're welcome. But now you do owe me dinner." Angela smiled up at tall young man towering over her. "You did mention tapas I think."

"I certainly did. There's a new place not far from here. Shall we walk?"

"Sure, but I'll have to take five steps to your two." She tucked her hand under Pete's arm and laughed. "This is so you won't lose me."

"Never fear. I've got you covered." They left the laboratory followed by a sour look from of one of Angela's fellow technicians.

Fifteen minutes later they entered Jaleo, already crowded with young people bent on starting their hump-day night, partying at one of the newest and most popular spots in downtown DC. Pete was able to find room at the end of one of the stand-up tables, and the harried waitress took his order for two mojitos as she dropped a pair of menus in front of them. Pete fished his own cell phone from his pocket, smiled ruefully at his companion, and motioned toward the men's room. "I've got to call the boss and tell him what you've done for us. Should only take a couple of minutes."

Angela nodded. "Go ahead. I'm okay here."

"Thanks. Be right back." Pete wound his way through the crowd and into the men's room. He dialed Jack Frazier's number. "Boss, got a lead on the prints. Thomas Reed, an attorney who probably works with Karin. His prints were on the glass. He must have been in her apartment sometime before she left Monday night. What do you want me to do now?"

"Nothing more right now, but stay loose. I may have to call you back. Where are you?"

"I'm at Jaleo with the FBI tech that ran the prints for us. I promised to buy her dinner if she could get 'em done today. She's a knockout, boss. Cute as hell."

Frazier grunted, "Aren't they all. Don't get too carried away. I may still need you tonight."

"Roger that. Call me if you need me." Pete disconnected and went back to the table where Angela was fending off two yuppie types who were trying to hit on her. Pete walked up behind them and cleared his throat. "The lady's with me, fellas. Thanks for looking out for her."

One of them spun around and found himself eye-to-eye with the breast pocket of Pete's sport jacket. He looked up and found his voice. "Sorry, man. No offense." He and his partner backed away and disappeared into the crowd at the bar.

Pete called after them as they left, "None taken. Have a nice evening." Then he leaned down to Angela. "Sorry. You all right? You looked as though you were taking care of those guys without any needing any help from me."

The young woman grinned. "Believe it or not, I'm used to it. And it doesn't bother me. Sometimes it's fun to play with them for a while."

The waitress deposited their drinks on the table and said she'd be back to take their order. Pete picked up his mojito. "Cheers. And I do believe guys try that a lot." He sipped his drink as he watched her. "Steady boyfriend?"

"No one special at the moment. How about you?" She blushed. "I mean, do you have a girlfriend, not a boyfriend."

"No to both sexes," Pete laughed. "Now tell me where you're from, and how did you wind up in a place like the FBI lab?"

"California originally. When I graduated from Stanford, I answered an ad, and I've been with the bureau for the last five years. After training, I was assigned to the lab. It's a three-year tour, so I'll probably go somewhere else next spring. I'm hoping for a field office somewhere where it's nice and warm. Maybe like Florida or Hawaii. I really hate cold weather." She took a sip of her drink and looked at him appraisingly as if deciding whether or not to tell him more. "My dad was in the Vietnam War, on the other side. He deserted from the North Vietnamese army and wound up in Thailand. My mom's Thai, so I'm kind of mixed. Eventually, they came to the States. Dad and Mom have a grocery store in Bakersfield, and I was born there." She sipped her mojito again. "Now it's your turn."

"Nothing much very exciting to tell. Born and raised in western North Dakota. Managed to swing an appointment to the Air Force Academy, played a little basketball, completed my required service, and got recruited by the Company eight years ago."

"Were you a pilot? I always wanted to get my license and maybe fly helicopters."

"No. I majored in political science and history, so I didn't opt for flight training after the academy. I'm six feet five and a little claustrophobic in the cockpit of a fighter. Wound up spending my time in the Office of Special Investigations, doing routine investigative work. Some of that stuff took place in Iraq and certain South American countries, which is how I wound up working for the Company."

Angela laughed. "I bet I'd fit in a cockpit. I'm five two, almost. My roommate, Melissa Rogers, is five ten. She played basketball at some college in New England someplace. She works over at DEA now. We've been sharing an apartment for a couple of years. You'd like her."

The waitress came back, and they ordered another drink and a mixed selection of the Spanish equivalent of appetizers.

Conversation lagged while they watched the crowd grow and waited for their order. Pete hoped that Jack wouldn't have to call him back this evening. Angela was easy to talk with, and he was more comfortable with her than he had been with any woman in a long time. But he had the feeling that it wouldn't last.

Thirty minutes later, just as they were finishing the tapas, his cell phone vibrated. He got it out before it rang and saw that it was Jack Frazier. "I'm here, boss. What's up."

"I need you in the office early in the morning. Around seven ought to do it. You okay with that?"

"No problem. I'll see you then." Pete dropped the phone back in his pocket and smiled at Angela. "Going to be short night, I'm afraid. The boss wants me in early, so I guess we'll have to call it quits pretty soon. I'm sorry."

The girl smiled back. "That's all right. I need to be in early anyway. I have to work tomorrow too. But I do have Friday off. Maybe we could do this again sometime when our jobs don't interfere. I've had a good time tonight."

"You bet we will. Perhaps this coming weekend if you're free." Pete was grinning foolishly. "Let me get you a cab. I've got your number at the lab, but if you'll give me your cell number, I'll call you tomorrow. Maybe we can get together during the day on Friday if that's all right."

"Sure. I'll be looking forward to it."

# Chapter 8

Wednesday, 8:00 p.m.

At eight o'clock, the bar on the roof of the Intercontinental Hotel was a busy place. Most of the tables were occupied by Pakistani business types, some with wives or girlfriends, but there were also a number of tourists. Even though the big room was air-conditioned, many of the customers were sweating in their suits and ties. Deke sympathized with them, knowing that he couldn't take his jacket off no matter how hot it was.

He looked for the newspaper reader while he searched for an empty table. The man wasn't in the crowd. Deke found an empty two-person table and grabbed it just before one of the local business types got to it, earning a nasty look and a mumbled curse in Urdu. Deke shrugged as he sat down, and a waiter instantly appeared, dropped a coaster in front of him, and asked for his order. He thought about a martini—James Bond wasn't the only spook who liked 'em—but settled for a bourbon and water. He was careful to specify *bourbon*. If he had said *whiskey*, the waiter would have brought Scotch. The English influence, he supposed.

His table was against the outside wall, and the big plate-glass windows offered a beautiful view of midtown Karachi. The bright glare of multicolored neon and the head and taillights of the early evening traffic combined to make a pleasant sight. While Deke sipped his drink and appeared to be looking out at the city, he was really watching the reflections of the people in the room, looking for the man he suspected was Faraz.

Deke's thoughts turned to Karin. She was too well organized and controlled to just disappear. Although she was in her midthirties, she looked several years younger. Her ash-blonde hair, pale-blue eyes, and trim, athletic figure bespoke her Norwegian heritage. Originally from

Michigan's Upper Peninsula, she was a graduate of that state's university. She had clerked for Justice Callahan of the Supreme Court and had also been in private practice for a couple of years before going to work for the attorney general. Karin and Deke had been doing dinner and theater dates for nearly two years, with an occasional sleepover whenever he was in town. Marriage had always looked like a possibility, but neither of them wanted to make that commitment while he worked for the Company. His marriage to Barbara had ended because of his job and the separations that came with it. But actually, Deke wasn't certain that marriage and the quiet life in a small town was what he was after, either.

"Mitchell?"

The voice that came from just over his right shoulder was soft and somehow familiar. Deke cursed himself for not paying more attention, but he didn't turn or respond, and the man spoke again.

"May I join you?"

"Certainly," Deke answered and looked up to see the little man with the scraggy mustache and the pockmarked face ease into the chair across from him.

"You are surprised to see me, no doubt. But I was delayed and unable to be here at eight o'clock as I had planned." The man grinned apologetically, showing his bad teeth again.

*Surprised* was an understatement. If this man was Faraz, he was also the Pakistani Inter-Services Intelligence agent from the lunchtime encounter at the Imperial. Deke decided to find out quickly.

"Where is Faraz?" He put the question directly and waited for the man's reaction. Deke was certain that the man knew who he was, and if that was true, then the guy also knew Deke was supposed to meet Faraz at eight o'clock.

"I am he." The ugly little man smiled again.

"And I know that because . . . ?" Deke let his voice trail off.

The man leaned forward, and Deke got an up-close and personal view of the pockmarks on his face and a whiff of the cheap aftershave he was wearing. He smiled once more, but there was no humor in it or in his tone. "I was to be paid a large sum of money for information which your country desires. I did not receive it. Your Mr. Scott did not meet with me in Peshawar as we had arranged." He sat back in the chair and signaled the waiter.

"And where is my Mr. Scott now?" Deke was pushing the man, and he knew that if he were to get any usable information from him, he would have to keep him on the defensive.

"I do not know. He was to meet me in Peshawar. He did not." The man ordered iced tea from the waiter. "It is still possible to complete our business if you can provide the required sum. Twenty million dollars was the figure quoted and agreed upon."

"Look, Faraz, if that is your name, I do not have access to that kind of money. And how do I know that you didn't receive the payment. All I have is your word on that. Until I talk to Cliff Scott, I can do nothing for you." Deke leaned back in his chair and signaled the waiter for a refill of his drink.

Faraz frowned. "Perhaps we can meet in Peshawar and together look for your Mr. Scott. He may be there still."

"It's possible, but I think he would have made contact with our people by now." Deke paused as his drink was delivered. "Unless he is unable to do that. Do your people have him somewhere? Did you turn him over to the Taliban?"

Faraz leaned forward. "I am not a member of that group. But I have connections to some of their people in that area. Even so, I do not think that they have Scott. I have not heard of him since he failed to meet with me. And if any of their leaders suspected that I was providing information to your government for money, I would be a dead man by now."

Deke believed that part of the man's story, but he still doubted that the money had not been delivered. "All right. I'll meet you at the Somerset Hotel in Peshawar on Friday. Ask for me at the desk. They'll know how to reach me."

"Very well, Mr. Mitchell. I will see you then." The small man rose, dropped some coins on the table, and headed for the door. Deke watched him closely but couldn't tell if he signaled anyone else in the room. Deke reasoned that Faraz probably had come with another agent and would put a tail on him, but he knew it would be impossible to pick such a man out in the crowded bar. He would just have to watch his back when he left.

He had settled back and picked up his drink again when he noticed the two English women at a table across the room.

*Now there's a coincidence*, he thought. He signaled the waiter and told him to take fresh drinks to the two young women. Deke watched as the drinks were delivered, and the two looked around to see who had sent them. They saw him and waved and then motioned for him to join them. *All right*, he mused, *let's see where this goes.*

Taking his drink with him, he made his way through the busy room.

"Good evening, ladies. I see you found a way to sample some of Karachi's night life. May I join you?" This last was superfluous; they clearly expected him to sit down.

The brunette, Elizabeth, spoke first. "Please do sit down. And thank you for the drink. A lovely room, isn't it?"

"Yes. I like it. Not too noisy, so conversations are possible. Did you find a decent restaurant tonight?"

Patricia, blonde and the shorter, more buxom of the pair, answered, "We did. A small, very clean place just a few doors from here. Excellent chicken curry. I think it was called "Tandoori". Have you been there?" She leaned forward toward Deke, focusing on him totally while her companion sat back and watched.

Deke finished his drink and caught the waiter's eye, indicating he wanted a refill, before he answered. "No, I don't think I've tried that one. There are a lot of good places here, and we contractors tend to stick to the same ones." He turned to Elizabeth. "So how long a holiday do you have? You said you were just passing through. Where are you going from here?"

"We can only stay in Pakistan for four more days. Actually, we were thinking of going up north, to the Khyber Pass if possible. We British have such a rich tradition in that area, and we would love to see the regimental crest markers that they say are all along the road to the pass. Do you think that's a good idea at this time? Would we have trouble with the military?"

*Another coincidence*, he thought. "I really don't know what the military situation is in the North-West Frontier. There are rumors of al-Qaeda and Taliban groups coming and going across the border, and I think the government is discouraging tourists from going anywhere north or west of Peshawar." Deke hoped that he had discouraged them.

The little blonde spoke up, "Oh, dear. I teach history, and I had so hoped to be able to tell my students that I had actually been there. It's so much better when we can speak from our own experiences, don't you agree?"

"I certainly do." Deke smiled. "And the more experiences, the better."

The girl blushed, her peaches-and-cream complexion turning a soft shade of pink, and smiled back. Her hand brushed his as she reached for a book of matches lying in the middle of the small table. Elizabeth frowned and stood up, pushing her chair back. "Well," she said, "I think I shall go back to the hotel. It's been a tiring day after all." She looked down at Patricia. "You should stay. You've hardly touched your drink." Turning to Deke, she spoke again, "You'll see that Pat gets home all right, won't you?" It seemed to him that it was more of a command than a question.

He watched her for a moment as she made her way to the exit. Then he turned back to the blonde. "She's right. You haven't touched your drink." He waited to see how she would respond.

"Oh, I really don't drink very much. Alcohol sometimes affects me in strange ways." She smiled and Deke recognized the line as a come-on, so he played along. *I'm pretty sure she and her partner are MI6. She's being too coy. Wonder what their game is?*

"You mean that you take your clothes off and dance on the tables? Or something better than that?" *There,* he thought, *that should give her an opening for whatever she wants to say.*

Patricia blushed again. "Well, not exactly like that, but they do say that too much alcohol will lower one's inhibitions. Do you think that's true?" She was being coy again.

"I don't know. Why don't we have another drink and see?" He moved his chair closer to hers. "I'm only kidding, of course."

"Are you married, David? Or do you have someone?" He noted that she had remembered his first name. Still, her questions were somewhat of a surprise to him, and he searched for an answer.

"Not married anymore, but I do have someone in the States that I'm fairly serious about."

"Fairly serious? What does that mean? I would think that you either are serious about someone or you are not. And you strike me as a very serious man." She sat back and sipped her drink. "Will you marry?"

"I honestly don't know yet. When I get back there, we'll see if that's what we want to do." Deke realized that what he had said was true. He took a big swallow of his drink and put that thought out of his mind. *Later,* he told himself, *I'll think about that when all this is over and I get back to DC.* He smiled at the girl sitting with him. "What say I take you back to your hotel? I hate to break this up, but I do have an early meeting in the morning."

"Of course, I should be getting back. Elizabeth will be wondering what we're up to."

Deke stood up and waved at the waiter who came immediately with his check. After handing the man a five-hundred-rupee note, he extended his hand to Patricia and then held her arm as they maneuvered through the tables toward the door. They had nearly reached the exit when the newspaper reader stepped in front of them. Deke's hand automatically went into his coat, reaching for the Glock, but the man put both of his hands in front of his chest and shook his head, showing that he wasn't armed. Deke dropped his hand to his side, and the man pulled an envelope from his breast pocket, handed it to him, nodded, and walked away.

Patricia turned to face Deke. "Wasn't that man at the Imperial Hotel this morning? What did he want with you?" She looked after the man as he threaded his way through the tables and went out the door at the far side of the bar.

Deke looked down at the envelope in his hand. It was cheap hotel stationery with no name on the front or back. *So, if the other guy was Faraz, who the hell are you. And what do you want with me?*

He took the girl by the arm and said, "Let's get you back to our hotel. This is just some business. Heck of a way to deliver invoices for supplies." He shrugged. "But that's the way they do things here sometimes." Deke knew she didn't believe a word of what he was saying, but he had no way out.

When they got back to the Imperial, Deke rode up to the fifth floor with Patricia and walked her to the door of her room. "Well, good night. Hope you have a pleasant stay here or up north if you go there." He started to turn away when she put her hand on his arm.

"I'd invite you in for a night cap if I wasn't sharing the room with Elizabeth."

Deke looked down at her and smiled slightly. "And in other circumstances, I might accept the invitation. Perhaps some other time." He didn't look back as he walked away toward the elevator, and after what seemed like a long time, he heard her open her door and go inside. Once in the elevator, Deke thought about what had just happened. *She's cute, and it might be fun to play, but I can't do that to Karin. I really need to see her. Or talk to her. It's only been three days since we had lunch together, and I miss her already.* He shook his head. *It must be love.*

# Chapter 9

Wednesday, 10:38 p.m.

When Karin opened her eyes, she could see nothing of her surroundings. Wherever she was, it was pitch-black. Her head pounded furiously, and she thought for a moment that she would vomit, but she forced herself to lie still until the nausea passed. She squeezed her eyes shut, willing herself to be calm. It was easier to think when she could stay within herself. She realized that she was on a bed or cot of some kind and that she was fully clothed and covered with blankets. *How did I get here? And where am I?* Her memory was distorted and jumbled. She recalled that she and Tom Reed had been somewhere having dinner. *Why was I with him? What happened to me?* She was exhausted and drifted off to sleep again.

Karin was stiff, and her body ached from lying in one position for so long the next time she regained consciousness. She tried to move her arms and found that her right wrist was handcuffed to the rail of the iron bedstead. The cuff was tight, and the edge of it cut into her wrist, but her hand began tingling as the feeling came back when she moved. She opened her eyes again. The room was so dark that she couldn't see any other furnishings, nor could she tell if there was a window. She tried to move around on the bed and sit up. She couldn't do that either. Her left ankle was also cuffed to the bed frame. She felt fear for the first time. Whoever had left her in this place had meant for her to stay put. Another memory surged up. Someone had given her a drink of water from a plastic bottle. *Who did that? And when? How long have I been wherever this is?* The nausea came back, and this time she did throw up, managing to get her head over the side of the bed just in time.

She was so tired and weak that she couldn't think straight. The fear gave way to the drugs, and she drifted off to sleep again as the GHB continued to work on her weakened system.

# Chapter 10

The traffic was light, and Pete was making good time around the beltway. The little strip mall that housed the RECOM office was just off Route 50 in Chantilly, a fairly long way out of the city but a truly good place to stay out of the public eye. He turned off the highway, pulled into the parking area, and eased into a vacant spot in front of the all-night Laundromat. The RECOM office was sandwiched between it and an office supply store. Jack Frazier's custom van was in the parking lot, and he was waiting in front of Pete's cube.

"Good morning, Sunshine. Had a nice night?" Jack turned his wheelchair around and headed for his own office.

"The young lady from the FBI lab and I had a swell time. Drinks and dinner, and then I put her in a cab for home. Wish it could have lasted longer."

Frazier's chair spun back around. "Are you kidding me? That's all?" He laughed and then shook his head. "Sorry I spoiled your plans." He laughed again. "I think."

"No problem. I'm going to see her again pretty soon. Now, what's up for this morning?"

Frazier settled himself behind his desk and motioned for Pete to sit in the only other chair in the office. "We know Reed was in the apartment. But we don't know when. He could have been there any time before Monday, or it could have been that evening. Was there anything else that you saw that might help?"

Pete thought for a minute and then remembered the flowers. "There was a bouquet of roses on the coffee table that might have been there a day or so. Maybe Reed brought the flowers to her that day." He waited a minute. "And there was still some water in the bottom of that glass. Smelled like Scotch. Could have been a melted ice cube from his drink."

Frazier nodded. "That's good. Go back over there and collect the flowers. Maybe you can find out where they came from. Take another look around. Talk to the neighbors if you can do that without causing a problem. Someone might have seen Reed and Karin together."

"Her car was in its stall behind the apartment. I'll find out what Reed drives. If he was there on Monday, maybe someone saw his car."

"Okay. We need to find out where he is and what he is doing. See if you can pick him up and tail him after you go through Karin's apartment again. I really doubt that he had anything to do with her disappearing. He's just an attorney in the AG's office and doesn't fit any sort of profile of a tough guy. They both work for the AG, so maybe it was just some business thing. Anyway, check out the apartment again, and if you need help with the tail, call me and I'll try to get someone for you." Frazier hesitated. "Don't know who that might be right now. I want to keep this in-house if we can. Langley doesn't have to know what we're doing. Not sure they'd appreciate our using Company resources for a private matter."

Pete straightened up in his chair. "Will they get a report from the FBI? I know Angela had to account for her time and for accessing the data bank."

Frazier thought for a minute. "Yeah, they'll get one eventually. All of this should be long over by then. Those things move through the system slowly. Anyway, I'll probably be able to explain that away without any trouble." He wheeled back around to the front of the desk. "Pete, we've got to find Karin before Deke comes back from Pakistan. He's told me that he's continued to try and call her without any luck, and he's pretty worried."

Pete stood up. "I'll go back to Karin's place right now. Do you want me to call you if I find anything else?"

"No. Just follow up on whatever you think is a good lead. I'll give you a call later. Good luck."

The drive back to Karin's apartment in Georgetown took a little longer since traffic had picked up as people headed into their jobs in the nation's capital from the surrounding suburbs. Route 50 was its usual nightmare of stop-and-go traffic. The weather was mild for the end of September, and Pete knew downtown DC would be crawling with end-of-summer tourists and the lucky locals who could get out to enjoy it. He wished he could go up to Baltimore and spend some time on his boat. He hoped that the weather would hold for a few more weeks and thought maybe Angela might enjoy a day on the water too.

Once again he followed a tenant into Karin's building and soon found himself in her apartment. Nothing had changed, and there was a slight musty smell from the decaying flowers on the coffee table. He moved them aside and saw that Karin's cell phone had been lying under the bouquet. He picked it up and realized that it had been turned off. He switched it on and noted the number of missed calls that were registered. He knew Deke's cell number and saw that all the calls since Monday night were from him. He switched the phone off again, put it in a small plastic bag, and slipped it into his pocket. Why, he wondered, would she have left her cell phone if she was traveling? He examined the flowers again. There was a small card tucked in among the thorny stems. "Wyndham Florists." The address and phone number were also given. When he left the apartment, he looked for any of Karin's neighbors that might be around, but he found no one to talk to.

Locating the florist shop was easy, but finding a place to park his Dodge Ram pickup nearby proved to be a problem. Pete finally found a spot around the corner from the shop, and carrying the now-wilted roses, he walked the half a block.

"Can I help you, sir?" The young woman behind the counter eyed the bouquet apprehensively as Pete came through the door.

"I believe these came from this shop, ma'am." Pete smiled at her and laid the bouquet on the counter, "I wonder if you could tell me when they were purchased. And by whom?" he added as if it were an afterthought.

"Well, I don't know. They certainly could have used some water after they left our shop." She bristled a little. "They could be a week old or more."

"No, ma'am. I believe they were bought sometime last Monday. Could you check that for me, please?" He didn't want to show his ID card to the woman and hoped she would just do as he asked.

"Monday you say? Let me look." She dug into a drawer under the counter and came up with a sheaf of receipts. She thumbed through them and then paused, "We don't sell many roses during the week usually. But there were four dozen sold that day." She looked at Pete again. "I don't know if I should tell you who bought them. Isn't that illegal or something?"

Pete decided to bluff. "This is a police matter. Since you're neither a lawyer nor a priest, the information on those receipts is not privileged. Just let me see the four names, and I promise you no one will ever know you helped the department."

"Well, okay." She slid the four receipts across the counter, turning them so Pete could read the names. Tom Reed's signature was on the credit card form stapled to the second one. The time of the sale was listed as 3:45 p.m., Monday, September 26, 2005.

Pete pushed the receipts back to the girl. "Thank you very much. You've been a great help to us today." He looked again at the wilted roses, smiled, and said, "I'm sure these were beautiful when they left your store. Thank you again."

Back in his truck, he decided to call Frazier after all. When his boss came on the line, Pete told him what he's found out about the flowers. "And I found Karin's cell phone too. Do you want me to bring it in or what? It's been turned off since Monday, and Deke's made a ton of calls to it."

"No. Hang on to it until tomorrow. And leave it turned off. I'll tell Deke we've got it, so he doesn't keep trying to call her. Now we know that Reed was in the apartment late Monday afternoon. Go see if you can find him and start tailing him as soon as you can. Call again when you've got him."

# Chapter 11

Reed negotiated the last turn off Route 50 onto State Route 29 toward Slanesville, West Virginia, and slowed down as an empty ten-wheeler coal truck pulled onto the road ahead of his Mercedes. Robert Chilton moved impatiently in the passenger seat. "How long is this going to take, Reed? I thought you said it was an easy drive."

"More traffic than I expected this morning. I think the early deer hunting season starts next weekend up here. Some of these people may be scouting." He stopped. "God, I hope no hunters go nosing around that old camp. It's posted as government property, but these rednecks don't respect signs all that much."

"You said it was a private area and that it was safe. What are you going to do if the girl is found?" Chilton was obviously putting all the problems on Reed.

Reed sped up and passed the empty truck. *Why is that my problem? I came back up here yesterday and made sure she couldn't get away. That's all I'm going to do.* He began looking for the turn that would take them onto the dirt road that led down off the mountain to the camp on the South Fork of the Potomac River. Spotting it, he signaled and made the right turn, wincing as the big Mercedes bounced over the low mound of dirt meant to discourage traffic. For the first mile or so, there were a few cabins in the woods along the road, but after that there was no evidence of anyone being in the area.

"Almost there." Reed muscled the big car through a patch of soft sand, and they dropped off the last little hill and onto the flat that contained the buildings of the old camp. Pulling past the shooting range and coming to a stop in front of the lodge, he killed the engine. "She's locked in the back bedroom."

Chilton climbed out of the car, slammed the door, and quickly mounted the three steps to the porch of the old lodge building while Reed was coming around the front of the vehicle. "Well, open the damn door."

Reed pushed past him and unlocked the door, shoved it open, and stepped back so the older man could enter first. They moved through the large central room filled with furniture protected by canvas and linen dust covers. To the left was a kitchen, and on the right, a short hallway led to a pair of bedrooms and a bathroom. Reed fumbled for the key to the far one and unlocked the door for Chilton. The older man entered and stopped in the middle of the room. He choked and coughed as the smell of dried vomit struck him. He pulled a handkerchief from his pocket and covered his nose and mouth.

Karin lay on the single bed and was covered by a blanket and a down comforter. Her slow, shallow breathing told them she was alive but either asleep or still unconscious. Reed spoke, "It doesn't look like she's moved since I left yesterday." He moved to the side of the bed and made sure that the handcuffs were still locked and that she couldn't get up. "I dissolved some phenobarbital in the water and forced her to drink it when I came back up here. I don't know how long that other stuff is supposed to last, but the phenobarb will keep her knocked out for a while longer."

"You really did a job on her, Reed. With that stuff and GHB in her system, she may never wake up."

Reed turned on him. "Damn it. You didn't tell me how much of that GHB to use to just make her sick. I never used that stuff before. This is your fault."

Chilton backed away from the bed. "Oh, calm down. It isn't going to make any difference. She'll be taken care of tomorrow or sometime this weekend at the latest. I've contacted some people to handle that for us. But they can't be here until Friday or Saturday night." He turned toward the door. "You'll have to come back up here with them to get her."

Reed turned to stare at the older man. "What are you talking about? I'm not coming up here with whoever you hired to kill her. I'm not a murderer. I'm all through with her now."

Chilton spun around. "You're right, Tom. You're not a killer. You're a kidnapper." His voice took on an angry edge. "And you will do exactly

47

what I tell you to do if you want to stay alive and out of jail. Do you understand me?" He turned away and headed for the bedroom door.

Reed stood still for a moment, absorbing the man's words and processing the threat they implied. Then he tucked the blanket up under Karin's chin again. He paused at the door and looked back at the woman chained to the bed. *I am sorry about this, and I wish there was some other way. But Chilton's right: I am in too deep to bail out now.* Just as he closed the door to lock it and follow the big man out through the empty lodge, he thought he saw her move. He didn't know how long Karin could last without food or water, but he thought that she would still be alive on Saturday.

# Chapter 12

The flight from Karachi to Peshawar was uneventful, even in the antiquated aircraft that were now being used by Pakistan International Airlines. The old airplanes were well worn and seeing hard usage since the wars in Iraq and Afghanistan had started. The air traffic demands were so heavy that PIA had pulled several old, well-used aircraft out of mothballs and was using them for internal flights. Deke spent the airtime trying to decipher the contents of the envelope the newspaper reader had passed to him.

The half sheet of note paper inside contained a hand-printed, cryptic message: "Faraz 3/agent Careful." The note had been crumpled and then smoothed out before being placed in the envelope. Deke was puzzled. Did the note indicate a meeting time? Or did "3/agent" mean something else? Deke wondered if the note's deliverer was also an al-Qaeda member or if he was one of the good guys. Perhaps Ahmed Kahn could help him figure that out.

He took a taxi to the Somerset Hotel as soon as he could get away from the crowded airport. The bar was empty except for the tall Sikh bartender. Ahmed Kahn was at least two inches taller and sixty pounds heavier than Deke, big, even for a Sikh. Deke approached the bar, placed his hands together and said, "Sat Sri Akal," the traditional Sikh greeting. The big man grinned broadly and replied in kind. Deke showed him his passport. Jamie Wilson had already contacted Kahn, so he was expected. While he sipped a cold Perrier, Deke told him that he was looking for Cliff Scott. Ahmed promised to check with some of his own sources at once and try to find out whether or not Scott had been in Peshawar.

Deke booked a room and called Jamie Wilson as soon as he got upstairs, "I'm in Peshawar. Ahmed Kahn is checking to see if Scott was here."

"All right. I'll come over to Peshawar this evening, and we can meet when I get to the hotel. Anything else?"

"Yeah. This Faraz is the same guy that we saw in the hotel. The little ugly guy with the Pak security ID. A double agent maybe? Maybe even a triple. Or just a hustler? I got a note from the guy they were hunting. I'll show it to you tonight." Deke paused. "Anything you want me to do with him if I find him?"

"Crap. If he's a double that's a complication we don't need. Just play it by ear. Do whatever you have to. I'll see you later tonight."

"Okay." Deke switched off his cell phone and retrieved the Glock from its hiding place in his luggage. He donned the holster and tucked the pistol away. A few minutes later, he walked back into the bar.

"Some news, sir," Ahmed greeted him at the door. "Mr. Scott was here but left for Kohat, where they make the guns. That was over a week ago. He has not returned to Peshawar as far as my sources can determine. And he has not been seen in Kohat."

"That's not that far from here as I remember." Deke was certain that they could pick up Scott's trail in Kohat, or at least find out if he had met someone there. "Can you get us a car?"

"I will get a car for us within the hour. We can leave as soon as you like. I have already arranged for someone to replace me, so I may leave the hotel."

"Let's do it, then. The sooner we find out what's happened to Cliff, the sooner we'll know where the money went. I'll wait for you in my room."

Ahmed Khan was as good as his word. He returned to the hotel in less than an hour with a beat-up, 80-something, four-door Toyota sedan. They crowded into the front seat, leaving very little room. Toyotas weren't built for men as large as they. The drive to the town of Kohat took a little over two hours on the badly maintained highway now crowded with garishly painted and decorated diesel trucks driven by Pakistanis with a death wish. Or so it seemed to Deke as they weaved their way through the traffic and around the potholes. "Where did you find this car, Ahmed? In a junk yard?"

The big Sikh laughed. "No, sir. It belongs to my wife's cousin. He was reluctant to let me borrow it for fear that it would be damaged in some way. As you can see, he keeps it in showroom condition."

Deke glanced at the torn headliner and badly stained seats. "Oh, I can tell that he is very proud of it. What does this cousin do for a living?"

Ahmed laughed again as he swerved to avoid a sheep that had run onto the road. "He is a farmer, and this car is his tractor and his truck. Yesterday he took his sheep to market." He sniffed loudly. "As you can surely tell."

Deke grunted and smiled. "And he must let his donkey sleep in it too. It smells like a stable."

Kohat was much as Deke remembered. Swollen now with refugees and Pakistani soldiers, it still was mostly a collection of open-fronted shops selling guns and gun parts. The main industry of the town was the production of cheap firearms, most of which were made by hand with primitive tools. The resulting weapons were sometimes more dangerous for the user than for the intended target.

Deke and Ahmed pulled up in front of the one combination hotel and restaurant on the dusty main street. Ahmed went inside to speak to the desk clerk, and Deke stood on the broad hotel veranda and watched as a gun buyer came out of an open-fronted shop next door with a rifle and three cartridges. The rifle was an exact copy of a .303 British Enfield Mark IV. Deke knew there was a local custom that mandated that if the weapon one was considering didn't blow up or malfunction in some other way after three shots, it was a sale. In the gathering dusk, he could see and hear other sales being completed in the same way up and down the street. Shaking his head, he turned and entered the hotel as the first shot rang out from the street.

Ahmed stepped away from the clerk's desk and came to him. "We must go to a restaurant in the old section of the city. Mr. Scott was last seen there."

"All right. Do we know whom to talk with there?" Deke asked.

"The owner is an Afghan from Kabul. It is believed that he has ties to the al-Qaeda or the Taliban in this area." The Sikh shrugged and smiled. "If he does, I believe I can get him to tell us what we wish to know." He placed his hand on the sheathed dagger at his waist.

The restaurant proved to be in a run-down building on a side street just behind the wall that separated the old section of Kohat from a somewhat newer commercial area. From the outside, it was difficult to tell that it was a restaurant at all. No sign graced the front, and the doorway was simply covered by long plastic strips which were intended to deter flies but was ineffective. Inside, they found a large room containing six tables covered with black and white checkered oilcloth. The smell of roasting meat and spices filled the room. When they entered, the only customer, a Pakistan Army sergeant, glanced up briefly and then returned to his bowl of curry. A waiter in dirty baggy trousers came from behind the small bar in the rear of the room. Ahmed asked him to find the owner, and he and Deke sat down at a table near the bar while the man went through a door in the back. He returned a few minutes later.

"Mr. Chandro is in the kitchen. He says for you to come there." The man motioned toward the door and went back to his seat behind the bar.

Deke got up from the table, and Ahmed followed him into the kitchen. A massive beehive oven dominated one end of the small room. Whole chickens were roasting on a long spit over a charcoal fire laid in a trench in the dirt floor near one wall. A leg of lamb hung above one end of the trench. Kettles of rice and vegetables were lined up on a low wooden bench against another wall. What appeared to be a wooden prep table held an assortment of pots, pans, and serving dishes. There was no sink, but a spigot over a large brass bowl served the purpose. Deke looked for another exit and saw that there was a doorway, also boasting the ineffective plastic strips, which led to the alley behind the building. The restaurant's owner, Chandro, was plastering uncooked chapattis against the smooth sides of the huge clay oven. A second man, hardly more than a boy and wearing dirty Levis and a torn black AC/DC T-shirt, slowly turned the spit over the charcoal-filled trench.

"You wished to speak with me?" Chandro was a short, muscular Afghan with the shoulders and arms of a wrestler. His shaved head showed grayish stubble in contrast to his black drooping moustache. A dirty smock hung over his soiled, baggy trousers. He didn't smile.

Deke locked eyes with him. "We're looking for information about an American who might have been here about a week ago. Can you help us?" He watched closely as the Afghan stooped, picked up a baked chapatti that had fallen to the floor, and tossed it onto a plate on the greasy prep table. As the man bent over, Deke spotted the telltale outline of the butt of a revolver which he had tucked into his waistband beneath the smock.

"I do not believe I can help you." The man smiled now and moved a step or two away from the oven, wiping his hands on the dirty smock.

"But perhaps I can." The voice was familiar.

Deke spun around. The man who called himself Faraz stood in the doorway leading to the alley, a pistol in his hand. He took a couple of steps into the kitchen. "You asked about your Mr. Scott. He was here a week ago, Mr. Mitchell." He stopped and then continued, "And he is still here in Kohat. He lies in the alley behind the wall of the mosque. I buried him there myself. And I shall do the same for you and this other infidel." He gestured toward Ahmed Kahn with the gun. "The two of you will disappear as easily and completely as he did." Faraz smiled again at Deke and raised the weapon.

# Chapter 13

The two rapid shots from the dining room doorway echoed loudly in the small room, and Faraz collapsed onto the kitchen's dirt floor. Deke had gone to one knee at the sound of the shots, drawing the Glock. Chandro reached under his smock and drew his revolver, but before he could aim accurately, Deke snapped a shot at him. The Afghan's round struck the dining room door frame, splintering it. Deke's aim was much better, and his bullet found its mark in the Afghan's chest. The man sagged against the beehive oven and slid to the floor where he died in a heap of partially cooked chapattis. Deke turned and looked for the third man. He was sprawled in the alley doorway with Ahmed's dagger resting against his throat. The big Sikh looked questioningly at Deke, who shook his head. There was no point in killing the young man if it wasn't necessary. Ahmed hauled him to his feet and shoved him through the back door. They heard the slap of his sandals as he ran down the cobbled alley. Deke turned to the dining room door.

Patricia stepped carefully into the kitchen, with her 9mm Walther PPK held in a steady two-handed grip, and pointed at Faraz. The mortally wounded man lay on the dirt floor, moaning softly and clutching his chest. Her first shot had hit him dead center just below his sternum; the second, an inch or so lower and to the right. His blood was puddling and beginning to sink into the dirt floor of the kitchen. Ahmed picked up Faraz's weapon and tucked it into his waistband and then retrieved the revolver that Chandro had been slow to draw. Deke knew Faraz was a dying man, but he needed information from him first.

"Your timing is excellent, Pat. Thanks." Deke grinned at the girl. "MI6, I presume."

The little blonde smiled back. "We suspected you had already figured that out. And you, of course, are not a contractor doing an airport job in Karachi. We knew that all along." She grinned and winked. "But it was fun to play the game. Elizabeth is covering the front, so we have time to do whatever is necessary." She nodded toward the man on the floor. "What do we do with him?"

"We let him die." Deke knelt beside Faraz. "Killed by an infidel." He paused. "And by a woman at that. I don't think there's a chance in hell that he'll make it to his paradise. But that's all right with me." Deke stood up and looked down at the dying man. "He does have an option, though, if he tells me what I want to know." Faraz stared up at him, with shadows of hatred and fear flitting across his pockmarked face. "I will tell you nothing." His voice was weak and his breathing shallow. "I will go to paradise. I have killed many infidels."

Deke smiled. "I'm not a student of the Quran, but I'm pretty sure that if you die at the hands of a woman, you're out of luck, my friend. And you will die very soon." He nodded toward Patricia. "And she is definitely a woman."

Patricia blushed and knelt down. "The bullet which will kill you did come from my pistol. And I will shoot you again to make certain that you die at my hands." She thumbed the Walther's hammer back.

"Say whatever prayer you want." She pointed the gun directly at the man's forehead. Faraz cringed and tried to move his head away, but Patricia kept the muzzle of the Walther pressed against his skin, now slick with perspiration.

"Wait," Deke spoke quickly. He looked down at Faraz. "I said you had an option. Tell me what I want to know, and I'll let Ahmed Kahn finish you." He looked toward the big Sikh, who showed the doomed man his dagger and smiled. "What'll it be?"

Faraz grunted and tried to sit up. "What do you want to know?" He tried but failed to spit in Patricia's direction. "I will not give her the honor of having killed me."

Patricia stood and backed off as Deke squatted beside the al-Qaeda agent. "You've already told us what happened to Scott. Now tell me where the bonds he delivered to you have gone."

Faraz's breath was coming in gasps now, and the color was rapidly draining from his sweat-streaked face. "London. They were sent to the Imam Akbar Hashemi." His voice was barely audible.

Deke looked at Patricia. "Do we know this Imam?"

She nodded. "I believe so. I'm sure we've been watching him and his mosque."

He turned back to the dying man. "One more thing. When did you meet with Scott? What day and what time?"

"Last week . . . Thursday . . . noon . . . here."

"How did you send the bonds to London?"

"Courier . . . bag."

Deke stood up and nodded to Ahmed Kahn. "Do whatever you need to, my friend. We will wait outside." He and Patricia went through the door into the dining room as the Sikh moved toward Faraz. "Do you have a car, Pat? We need to get back to Peshawar as soon as we can."

"Yes, it's outside. Elizabeth will drive."

The dining room was empty except for Elizabeth who was standing near the restaurant's entrance, with her pistol held at her side.

"What happened to the bartender? And the sergeant?" Deke looked around the room.

Elizabeth glanced toward the doorway. "The sergeant left when we came in, and the other one went out the door when Patricia fired."

Deke holstered his Glock. "Good. I doubt that we have to worry about either of them, or the shots. There's a lot of that going on outside anyway."

# Chapter 14

When Ahmed Khan came from the kitchen, his dagger was in its customary place in the ornate sheath at his waist. He nodded briefly to the two women and turned to face Deke.

"It is done. He has gone to his paradise, whatever that may be."

Deke moved forward and gripped the big Sikh by the arm. "Thank you, Ahmed. I will tell our people what you have done for us. Can you stay here until they can send someone to help recover Cliff Scott's body? They can probably be here tomorrow. Will you have any difficulty explaining any of this to the local authorities?"

"No. I believe I will be able to take care of any questions. My cousin is a sergeant of the Kohat police force. I do not think there will be a problem. I will stay here as long as necessary."

"Good. If you can use their weapons, you can have them. And thank you again." Deke turned to Elizabeth. "Where did you get the car in Peshawar?"

"The rental agency at the airport arranged it for us. Is that a problem?"

Deke shook his head. "Normally it wouldn't be. But up here everyone seems to be working for someone else." He turned back to Ahmed Kahn. "Can we trade cars with you? Will your wife's cousin object if we take his car back to Peshawar? We can leave it at the hotel for you."

"No, sir. He will not care." Ahmed hesitated and then smiled. "As long as you do not damage it further."

Deke laughed. "I don't think there is any danger of causing any more problems than it already has. Help us put these table coverings over the seats. Perhaps he will consider them a fair rental fee. You can bring the other car back when our people finish here, and they'll get someone to return it to the airport."

Ten minutes later, Deke and the two MI6 agents were in the beat-up Toyota on the road to Peshawar. Elizabeth drove carefully on the still crowded highway. The traffic had not let up, and the overloaded trucks, buses, and carts continued to stream in both directions.

"I'll let Jamie know the details of what happened when we get back to Peshawar, but I have to give him a quick heads-up now. He can send some people to Kohat to recover Cliff's body and clean up whatever mess is still there." Deke turned and looked at Patricia in the backseat. "Do you want him to tell your people what happened, or would you prefer to do that?"

"Go ahead and let him do it. I'm sure he is in contact with Edward Rook, our man in Islamabad. He's in Peshawar now, and we met with him at the airport. He's the one who told us that he thought you were going to Kohat. He was upset and didn't want us to follow you or try and make contact again, but I don't believe he knew why you were going there. We didn't know that either. We got to the hotel just as you were getting into this car with the Sikh, and we decided to follow you anyway." She sighed. "But since I fired my service weapon, I'll have to file a full report with him. I can wait a bit on that." She sighed again. "Mounds and mounds of paperwork." Then she brightened. "Do you go to London now? And can we go with you?"

Deke grinned. "Absolutely. I have to get those bonds back, and if that's where they went, that's where I have to go. Besides, you have to be there to save my life if it needs saving again." He smiled at the young woman, "Thank you for doing that, by the way. I owe you big time."

Patricia blushed. "No thanks are necessary. I believe they will let us go to London with you since MI6 also may have an interest in this imam Hashemi. Besides, it will be good to go home again for a bit."

Deke turned back to the front in time to see Elizabeth skillfully avoid a heavily overloaded donkey cart crowding its way onto the narrow highway. He pulled his cell phone from its holster on his belt and speed-dialed Jamie Wilson.

"Jamie. We had a bit of a problem in Kohat but managed to take care of it. I'll give you the details when we get to the hotel. Did you know that the Brits are involved in this?"

Wilson answered, "Yeah, their man in Islamabad gave me a quick briefing yesterday. They've got a couple of people in the area, but they're not interested in the bonds. Just trying to get info on some sort of operation that may involve something going on in London. At least that's what he told me, but he was pretty vague about it all. He's here in Peshawar now. Did you find the bonds? Or Cliff Scott?"

"No bonds here. They've been sent to London which is where we have to go ASAP. How soon can you get me and the two Brits out of here?" He hesitated a few seconds and then decided to tell Jamie the bad news. "Jamie, Cliff is dead, and Faraz told me he is buried by the mosque in Kohat. Faraz is also dead. I'll fill you in on the whole thing when we meet with you at the hotel."

"Sorry to hear about Cliff." Wilson thought for a few seconds. "I assume the two Brits are the guys Rook told me about. I may be able to get you all on an air force plane to Karachi later tonight, but you'll have to go commercial from there to London. I'll make some calls and try to set it up so you don't have much of a wait. I'm back in Peshawar, and if you have to, you can stay at the Somerset with me tonight."

"I've already booked a room, but that'll work. You may need to get a room for the Brits too. And just so you know, they are not guys. Two very nice young ladies. Whoever does their recruiting knows how to pick 'em."

"How do you always manage to wind up with good-looking women, Deke? I seem to remember something like that happened when we were in Istanbul a couple of years ago." He laughed. "Anyway, I'll take care of the rooms and see you at the hotel. Should know about the air force ride by the time you get here."

Deke hit the disconnect button on the phone and slumped back into the seat. All of a sudden he was exhausted. The past few days had taken their toll. He thought of Karin and then reached for the phone again but stopped. *I'll do that from the hotel when I have some private time,* he thought. He closed his eyes and leaned back against the headrest. Neither Patricia nor Elizabeth seemed inclined to talk, and he instinctively trusted Elizabeth's driving on the crowded highway. They were still more than an hour away from the hotel, and he thought maybe he could relax for that brief time.

Deke woke with a start when he felt the car come to a stop. A Pakistani policeman stood in front of a wooden barricade in the middle of the road and motioned for them to pull over to the side although he was allowing other vehicles to pass. Elizabeth looked at Deke. "Should we do anything special here? Why have they stopped us, do you think?"

"Don't know, but do whatever he says. I hope it's just a routine check of our papers." He carefully loosened the Glock in its holster. He wondered if someone in Kohat had tipped the police to what had happened there.

Another policeman, wearing more stripes on his sleeve, came to the driver's side window and bent down to look in. He smiled at Elizabeth, gave a half-hearted salute, and asked for her driver's license. She dug into her small bag and produced an international permit. Deke was surprised that she actually had one and then realized that she couldn't have rented the other car without one. The policeman took his time examining the permit and then asked for their passports. He took all of the documents over to an unmarked car parked behind the barricade, and handed them to someone in the rear seat. A few minutes later he returned with the papers and handed them back to Elizabeth before he turned and went back to the other car. "Now what do we do? I don't think this is just a routine stop, Agent Mitchell." Elizabeth was worried and looked anxiously at Deke and then at Patricia.

Deke tried to see whoever was in the backseat of the other car, but it was too far away and darkness was coming on. "I don't know. Look, he's coming back."

The policeman returned, saluted again, and looked at Deke and Patricia carefully before he thanked Elizabeth and told her to proceed. She put the beat-up car into gear and pulled back onto the highway. Deke heaved a sigh of relief and smiled at her. "Well done. Perhaps that was just a routine thing." He turned and looked past Patricia through the dirty rear window. "Oops. Maybe I spoke too soon. That car pulled out from behind the barricade, and they're following us. Be careful how you drive."

Elizabeth nodded and continued to drive cautiously until they reached the outskirts of Peshawar and turned onto the main road to the Somerset Hotel. They pulled up in front of the entrance, and Deke climbed out of the passenger seat. He watched as the black car slowly drove past and turned at the first intersection. He tried to see who the man in the rear seat was but couldn't quite make him out. *He looks a little like the guy from the Imperial. Maybe he was a cop.* He shrugged and turned to open the rear door for Patricia, holding his hand out to her as she swung her legs over the sill. She reached up to take his hand and hesitated, looking directly into his eyes. Her small hand was warm in his, and he felt his cheeks redden. They stood like that for a long moment and then she spoke.

"A gentleman. It's nice to meet one finally. Thank you." She squeezed his hand and came out of the car. Deke couldn't think of an appropriate response. At that moment, Jamie Wilson came down the hotel steps and saved him from further embarrassment.

# Chapter 15

Friday, 9:15 a.m.

An hour and a half out of Doha, Deke shifted his position in the not-so-plush coach seat of Qatar Airways flight 319 en route to London Heathrow. They had made their short stop in Doha on schedule, spending a little less than an hour on the ground. He was careful not to wake Patricia, who slept fitfully in the seat next to him. She had dozed through the flight from Karachi and the stop in Doha. Elizabeth was also asleep, leaning against the window. Deke always took an aisle seat if he could. They provided more space, and he could stretch his legs into the aisle once in a while. The three of them had spent the evening before in Jamie Wilson's room at the Somerset going through the day's events in great detail with him and Edward Rook, the MI6 liaison officer from Islamabad. Rook seemed exceptionally upset because Patricia killed the man known as Faraz. He made them repeat everything that was said and done in Kohat several times. Rook told them that he was not concerned with the missing bonds, declaring that it was a CIA problem and of no concern to Her Majesty's government. After a great deal of discussion, he had agreed to let Patricia and Elizabeth accompany Deke to London with the understanding that they would not participate in any attempt to recover the missing bonds. The two women were to report to their supervisor at MI6, file the requisite reports, and then wait for further orders. The two women were not happy with those instructions.

Patricia changed her position in the seat and leaned toward him, falling against his shoulder and putting her hand on his arm. He couldn't be certain she was really asleep as she snuggled against him. He could smell the faint aroma of the shampoo she had used when they had taken time to clean up at the hotel. He liked it, and then he was suddenly ashamed because he had momentarily forgotten Karin. Patricia was a very attractive young woman and obviously coming on to him. He cautiously changed his position again and signaled the flight attendant that he wanted a refill of his coffee. He considered a drink, maybe a Bloody Mary, but decided against it. They still had about six hours of flying time before they reached London. With the time difference, they would arrive at Heathrow just before ten in the morning, probably too early to be drinking. They had been up all night. Jamie had been able to arrange a ride for them on a USAF C-130 cargo flight from Peshawar to Karachi. They had left their Peshawar hotel around 1 a.m. and arrived in Karachi in plenty of time to catch their 6 a.m. Qatar Airways flight. The lack of sleep was beginning to take its toll on all of them, but Deke still couldn't settle down and nap. He sipped his fresh coffee and looked down at the little blonde sleeping against his arm with a faint smile on her full lips. *What if?* he mused. And again thoughts of Karin flooded over him. He now knew why he had been unable to contact her, but still didn't know where she was. Jack Frazier had told him about recovering her cell phone from the apartment but had been unable to tell him anything else the previous evening. Deke was certain that there would be some more information by the time they reached London. Jack seemed hopeful.

Deke knew that Jack was just as concerned as he was and would do his best to find out what was going on with Karin. He and Jack had been close friends for a long time. They had been recruited out of their colleges in the same year, he from the University of Texas and Jack from Florida State. They had trained together at Langley and Quantico and often worked together in the field. Both were experts on affairs in the Middle East. Their career paths followed parallel tracks until the day in 1997 when Jack had nearly been killed.

Deke changed his mind about the drink and asked the flight attendant for a Bloody Mary. He settled into a more comfortable position, again being careful not to wake Patricia, and thought back to that day in Beirut when he and Jack were attacked.

They had been in Beirut for nearly a week and taken care of some routine Company business. Assigned to RECOM at that time, their business in this case meant kidnapping and interrogating a leader of one of the local terrorist groups involved in an operation against Israel. The man was stubborn but eventually agreed to talk when faced with several unpleasant alternatives, and they got some very valuable information before turning him over to the Lebanese authorities for trial on whatever charges the local courts could dream up. On their way to the airport to make their flight back to Washington, a van cut them off and forced their driver to stop. A rocket-propelled grenade fired from an alley struck the left side of the car dead center. The blast flipped the vehicle over on its right side. Deke had been sitting on that side and was able to pull Jack through the shattered windshield before the car was engulfed in flames. He could do nothing for the driver who was dead behind the wheel. Deke suffered some minor cuts and bruises, but Jack's legs had been ruined, and his recovery was long and difficult. It was nearly three years before he came back as chief of RECOM, no longer fit for field duty.

Deke finished his drink and signaled the girl for another. Patricia stirred and sat up. She yawned, stretched and, eyeing Deke's fresh drink, said, "Ooh, that looks good. Could I have one of those, please?" The attendant nodded, smiled, and turned to the galley to mix another.

"Not too early in the day for you?" Deke grinned at his now wide-awake companion.

"Not after yesterday. Could really have used something to drink last evening, but no one offered." She stretched again. "Are all US Air Force aircraft as cold and noisy as that one was last night? I nearly froze to death until that nice sergeant brought me a blanket."

Deke laughed. "He'd have crawled under it with you if you'd asked him. Couldn't take his eyes off you. Those guys don't get many passengers as pretty as you two."

She accepted her drink from the attendant and took a sip. "That's better." Looking at Deke, she said, "Really. I just thought he was being sweet and kind to us. Do you think I'm pretty, David?"

"You might as well call me Deke like everyone else. And, yes, I think you are very attractive." He took a long pull at his drink and waited for her next move.

"Thank you. I was beginning to wonder. Why are you called *Deke*?"

"My initials are D. K., and for a long time, that's what my friends called me: *DeeKay*. Then it got shortened to *Deke*. That's what my close friends call me now."

She brightened, "And am I a close friend?"

"Anyone who saves my life is a close friend."

She turned away and then back again. "That's not what I meant. And you know it."

Deke looked at her. She was serious and a little bit angry at him. "Patricia, I'm sorry. I don't know what to do with you, or about you."

"That's all right. We really don't know each other." She took a drink of her Bloody Mary. "Tell me where you live in the States. Do you live in Washington?"

"Close. I have an apartment in Herndon. That's out near Dulles airport and not too far from the office where I work. How about you? In the city?"

She laughed. "No. The 'city' is a district of London. I live in the West End. I have a nice ground-floor flat and a bit of a garden to tend when I'm in town. Have you always lived in the East?"

"Since I joined the Company, but I have a little place down in Texas too. It's on the Gulf Coast between Corpus Christi and Brownsville, if you know where that is." Deke frowned. "I don't get to spend much time down there, but after this job, I'm going to the coast for a long stay. Maybe permanently, since I'm going to retire when I get back to the States."

"Retire? Goodness, I wouldn't think that you would want to do anything like that. Not at your age. How long have you been an agent?"

"Too long. Really, it's been twenty-five years since I joined the company. And I'm getting tired of it. Guess it's time I tried something new, or different." He looked at her closely, "How long have you worked for MI6?"

"Only a little over eight years. I finished school, and one of the professors seconded me to the service. I really like it. I enjoy the travel, and it's fun to pretend to be someone else now and then." She shrugged. "I really don't like the routine paperwork we have to do. And poring over ledgers all day for weeks on end is not much fun. That's what I do most of the time. I've become somewhat of an expert at analyzing and following money trails." She put her hand on his arm. "But this assignment has been really enjoyable." She frowned again. "Except for the shooting part. I really didn't like that."

Deke looked at her. "You handled it beautifully. Faraz certainly believed you would shoot him again. And so did I. You're a very good actress. Is that what you studied at school?"

"Oh Lord, no. I went to the London School of Economics. My degrees are in accounting and international trade. You must have gone to university, too. Where did you go?"

"University of Texas. My folks and I lived in San Antonio off and on for years. My dad was in the air force, and every time we came back from one of his overseas tours, we wound up there. I went to high school there, and Texas recruited me to play football. Dad wanted me to apply to the Air Force Academy, but I took the football scholarship at Texas instead. It's a good school, and I had a good time playing ball." He grinned. "Even managed to graduate. And then the Company recruited me, and the rest, as they say, is history."

"Does your family still live in Texas?"

"No. Dad was killed in a plane crash in 1978, and Mom died of cancer seven years ago."

Patricia took his hand. "I'm so sorry, Deke. Do you have brothers or sisters?"

He squeezed her hand, "No. I'm the spoiled only child." He laughed. "I guess that's the common belief, anyway. I really did have a great childhood. Lived in Germany and Okinawa. I even lived in London for a little while, but I was too young to appreciate it. Dad had some good assignments during his career." He disengaged his hand. "I do have an ex-wife and a son in college, but I don't see or hear much from either of them. We were divorced a long time ago."

She looked at him carefully. "I'm sorry. Divorces can be awfully hard on everyone."

"No. It's all right. We're still friendly, but we live on different coasts, and really in different worlds. My son and I are in contact occasionally, and we do see each other as often as we can arrange it." He signaled the attendant and ordered two more drinks. "Do your people live in London too?"

"No. They have a place in Cheltenham. My sister and her husband live there also. Dad works at GCHQ. Do you know what that is?"

"Yeah. I've been there a couple of times. It's a nice train trip up from London. There were some people out there that I knew pretty well: a couple of Russian linguists and an analyst I worked with once in Germany a long time ago. Nice guys and we had some good times after duty hours. We did some pub crawling in Cheltenham with some of the other people assigned there. Nice city."

"Dad's been there a long time and now is in charge of one of the divisions, cryptanalysis, I think. He wanted me to join GCHQ after school and was disappointed when MI6 took me. Mum didn't care either way.

She just wants me to get married and give her grandchildren." Patricia smiled up at him. "But I'm not nearly ready to do that just yet."

"And what does your boyfriend say about that? You do have one, don't you?" He pulled back a little and grinned at her. "Or maybe several. I'm thinking that a girl as good-looking as you would have to beat them off with a club."

Laughing, she said, "No one special right now, I'm afraid. I'm thirty-one, so maybe I'm destined to be an old maid. My mother certainly thinks so. She constantly throws single men at me, hoping I'll catch one of them. They're all very nice, of course, but I just haven't found the right one." She sighed, "Someday I'm certain I'll meet someone. I have plenty of time yet."

"I'll say amen to that. How about another Bloody Mary?"

# Chapter 16

Ellis Waverly, the director of the Central Intelligence Agency, leaned forward in his chair and folded his hands on Jack Frazier's desk. "Jack, what are you and your boys up to? Heard one of your people used the FBI lab downtown the other day. Is this something we should know about out at Langley?"

The director's unannounced visit to the RECOM office did not catch Jack Frazier completely by surprise. Like any good spook, Jack had his own internal pipeline into the Agency's headquarters, and he received a cryptic phone call twenty minutes before Waverly and his entourage came through the door in Chantilly. A report must have been sent from the FBI lab to the Agency about the fingerprint check. Now he was going to have to explain what he and Pete Sanders had been doing long before he had thought.

"Nothing pertaining to national security, Ellis. Just checking some fingerprints, so I didn't think the people out there should be bothered with it." Jack turned his wheelchair sideways to the desk. "Is there a problem? If you get a bill from the FBI, you can take it out of my budget."

Waverly wasn't amused. "Some sort of local case you're working on, Jack? I don't think we've sent anything down to you that involves any attorneys working in the attorney general's office." He stopped and locked eyes with Frazier. "How about telling me what's up with no bullshit added." The director settled back in the chair.

*Christ, what kind of report was that? And who sent it?* Jack had no clue, but he knew he would have to give up all the information he had. He turned to face his boss, "It's a personal thing, Ellis. Deke Mitchell's fiancée has gone missing. They were supposed to go to Texas this week on vacation, but she dropped out of sight last Monday night. As you know, Deke's in Pakistan, working Cliff Scott's disappearance and looking for the missing bonds. He's worried, and we're trying to find out what happened to his girl. All we know at the moment is that the attorney, Tom Reed, was in her apartment the day she vanished. I put Pete Sanders on it, since he was available." Jack leaned back, "That's it in a nutshell."

Waverly nodded. "All right. Why the FBI lab and not ours?"

"We thought it might be quicker, and besides, this is something that concerns one of our own and I didn't want everyone at the Farm looking over our shoulders."

"You and Mitchell go back a ways, don't you? Wasn't he with you in Beirut?" Waverly had been the director for not quite three years.

"Yeah. He saved my life there in '97." Jack paused. "Ellis, Deke is the best agent we've got in RECOM. Knows the Mid-East well but can, and has, worked everywhere."

"I know his record. I read his file a couple of weeks ago. Supposed to be retired as of today, isn't that right?"

"Yes, but we kept him on to handle this one last job, Operation Swift Mission. For some time now, I've tried to talk him into staying with us, but he says he's had enough. He's planning on going down to his place in Texas and chill out for a while. Maybe you could talk him into sticking around for a few more years. This al-Qaeda-Taliban thing is only going to get worse, and I believe you'll need a man like him for the next few years."

Waverly smiled. "We agree on that. Perhaps if I offered him a different job, he would reconsider retiring. What do you think would interest him? I don't believe he'd enjoy a desk job at Langley, do you?"

"Absolutely not. He's always been a field man, and he'd be totally wasted out there behind a desk." Jack paused and then leaned forward, looking directly at his boss. "Why don't you offer him my job? Put him in charge of RECOM. He could still do the field work if he was needed or wanted to, something I haven't been able to do since I've been here." He took a deep breath. "And besides, I think I'm ready to retire, too. I've worked for the Agency for twenty-five years, just like Deke, and it's probably time for me to hang it up and do something else." He sat back and waited for Waverly to speak.

Waverly leaned back in her chair and looked around the small office. "That might not be a bad idea. But I don't think we want to lose you either, so don't type up your resignation just yet. Let me think about it and see what options we have. I'll talk to some other people too. When is Mitchell due back?"

"He should be in London today, and it's possible they'll wrap things up by tomorrow night. I expect he'll catch the first flight out after that and could be here sometime Sunday if everything goes right. With your approval, Pete and I will keep working on the missing girl." He waited for the director's next comment.

"No. You do know you're out of line on that, don't you? Actually you've broken the law. The Agency is forbidden to spy on US citizens here at home." Waverly paused. "AG Marsh is pissed about this. And when she's not happy, nobody's happy. Do not involve the Agency in any more of this. Understood?"

"Yes, sir, but Pete's doing some follow-up today, and I'd like him to finish it up. If we turn up anything on the woman's disappearance, I will let you know immediately. Will that be all right?"

Waverly thought for a moment before he nodded and said, "All right, finish what you're doing. I'll call the AG and cool her off. But nothing else unless I okay it."

"That's fine, sir."

"Are you thinking the girl might have been kidnapped?" He laughed. "That's ridiculous. She probably just took off for her own reasons. Maybe she just got cold feet about going to Texas."

Jack rolled his chair around the desk as the director stood up. "Could be. But that's not like her." He shook hands with his boss and breathed a sigh of relief when the man disappeared through the front door.

*Now what?* He thought. *Do I really want to retire?*

# Chapter 17

Friday, 3:50 p.m.

Tom Reed turned off State Route 29 onto the county road that would take him to the Potomac. He saw the black pickup truck that was behind him go straight on through the crossroads. For a little while he had thought that the truck was following him, but now he decided that he was just being paranoid. He had planned on coming up here to check on Karin Jansen and try to give her some more phenobarbital but had not been able to get away until just before lunch. He really liked Karin, and even though she had rebuffed his advances in the past, he had always hoped that she would come around and become one of his conquests. Thinking about her, he had been unable to concentrate at the office, and telling his secretary that maybe he would be back later, he had taken off. Now he looked for the private dirt road that would take him down to the camp along the river.

A mile or so past the second crossroads, he turned right onto the now-familiar road and eased along the bluff until it dropped onto the flat containing the camp's buildings. When he entered the bedroom where he had locked Karin, he saw that the woman lay just as they had left her the day before. *She's dead*, was his first thought. Bending close to her mouth, he could barely feel her breath on his cheek. Karin's slow, deep breathing reassured him momentarily. He felt for her pulse and found it to be slow and steady but very weak. *How long can she last without food*, he wondered. *Perhaps Chilton just wanted her to starve to death. Maybe he really hasn't made any arrangements for someone to come up here and dispose of her. Well, I can't feed her, but I can give her some water.*

He picked up the bottle of water in which he had dissolved the phenobarb, and sitting on the edge of the bed, he lifted her up and poured a trickle of water into her mouth. Some of it ran down her chin and onto the blanket that covered her, but she convulsively swallowed most of it. She coughed, and he lifted her shoulders higher and pounded her on the back. He tried again and was able to get more of the drug-laced liquid down Karin's throat. Now that he knew that most of the water, and the drug, had gotten down, he felt better. She would sleep some more.

He laid her back down and covered her with the blanket and comforter again, making certain that the handcuffs were still tight. It was cool in the room, but he was sure that her covers were adequate. *All right, Karin, that's all I can do for you now. If those people show up, Chilton told me I would have to come back up here with them, so maybe I will see you again.* He looked down at the woman, *You know I really didn't want this to happen, but we couldn't take the risk that you would find out about Senator Whiting's illegal funding.*

He locked her in again and left the camp. Back on the county road, he considered going back to the office but decided against it. He remembered that he and Susan were invited to an after-theater cocktail party at the home of some friends later in the evening, but he was certain that if he could get back to the city, he would have time to spend a few minutes with Natalie, his most recent conquest and current partner in the latest of his extramarital affairs. He accelerated and then slowed as he came to the crossroads where Route 29 intersected. He'd have to hurry now. Turning right onto Route 29, he glanced quickly to his left and saw the black pickup again. *Hell, it's just a guy and his girl.* It was parked near the roadside produce stand just north of the crossroads. He floored the Mercedes and sped south. When he saw that the black truck was not following, he slowed to the speed limit and continued toward the city. *Relax. No one is following you, you idiot. You're being paranoid again.*

# Chapter 18

Friday, 3:50 p.m.

Pete drove carefully, keeping one or two vehicles between his truck and Tom Reed's Mercedes. He had picked up Reed's shiny white car when the attorney came out of the Department of Justice building just before noon. Reed had pointed his car west to Arlington and then onto Interstate 66. Pete had called Jack Frazier and was told to stay on their target and see where he was going.

Now they were west of Winchester on Route 50. Pete's truck was anything but inconspicuous, not the ideal vehicle for tailing someone. But he doubted that Reed would think he was being followed, and Pete was good at shadowing. He knew he wouldn't lose him.

"Where do you think he's going?" Angela's question broke the silence that had been building for the past fifteen minutes.

"I don't have a clue. But it's a nice day for a drive anyway." He smiled down at the girl in the seat next to him. She was leaning against the console that separated the two bucket seats in Pete's Dodge. Since it was her day off, he had invited her to go along when he tailed the attorney. She was an FBI agent, so he didn't believe it would be a problem. In fact, she could prove to be a great deal of help. Besides, she was pretty, and he wanted to spend some more time with her.

Reed turned north on Route 29 and continued toward the Maryland line. Pete wondered what interest he had in this area of small farms nestled in the wooded hills. The big Mercedes turned west on a no-name county road, and Pete went on past, pulling over when Reed's car went out of sight.

"We'll be spotted for sure if we follow him down that road. It was bad enough on Route 50, where traffic was light, and it got worse here on 29, but there's no traffic to hide in on that county road. We'll just have to wait and see if he comes back this way." Angela nodded and settled into the seat, tucking her legs up under her.

*Where the hell is he going? There's nothing up here but small farms and woods. I'll give him a half hour.* Pete turned the truck around and drove back to a roadside produce stand just north of the county road their target had taken. The half hour passed and he reconsidered opting to stay longer. His GPS and the map that he had showed the county road going on across the river and up toward Cumberland, but he doubted that Reed would take such an odd route to go there.

He turned to Angela. "How about we do some grocery shopping?"

They got out of the truck, and Pete spoke to the man at the stand, "Can you tell me where that road goes?"

"Sure. You can take it to get back over to route 28 and then up to Cumberland."

"Any side roads off from it? Or does it go straight through?"

"There are a few dirt roads that go off to the river and some cabins and an old government camp of some kind down there, but it isn't that far until it hits 28." The man looked at the girl browsing through the produce stacked on the rough wooden tables, and then turned back to Pete. "You headed that way?"

"No. We just wondered where it went. Good-looking apples you got here. Give us a couple pounds, and we'll be on our way." Pete paid for the apples, and they walked back to his truck.

When they were back in the truck, Angela said, "Maybe we should wait just a little longer. He hasn't been gone that long."

"You're right. I really doubt that he would take this route to Cumberland, so he's got to come back this way. Let's give him another half hour, and then I'll check in with the boss."

The Mercedes reappeared about twenty minutes later. It turned south and headed back the way they had come. *No point in following him home. I'll just see if I can find out where he's been.* Pete let the car get out of sight and then pulled onto the county blacktop. After nearly seven miles, he came to a crossroad. His map showed the road he was on continuing to the river, so he kept going west. A mile or so later, he came to a dirt road that led north toward the river. A faded wooden sign warned him that it was a private road and trespassers would be prosecuted. Pete drove on until he reached the bridge over the South Fork of the Potomac River. Deciding that Reed had not come that far, he turned around and started back. *The only place he could have gone is down that dirt road. Why would he do that?* Pete stopped on the shoulder opposite the road and called his boss. "Jack, I trailed Reed up here in the northeast corner of West Virginia, but I don't know what he was doing. I think he went down an old dirt road, but he's back on the highway now and probably headed back to the city. What do you want me to do?"

"Get back on him if you can, and if he goes home, come into the office. We can probably pinpoint where he went using satellite photos from the Company files."

"Roger that. There's a sign on the road that says it's private property. Maybe we can find out who owns it. A guy I talked to said there's some cabins and a government camp of some sort down by the river. Perhaps Reed went to one of those cabins or down to that camp."

"All right. Forget about picking him up again. Come on in."

Pete dropped Angela at a bar called The Back Yard, located about a mile from the RECOM office, promised to come back as soon as he could, and went to meet with his boss. When Pete got to the office, Jack was already looking at aerial and satellite photos of the camp area. Together, they pinpointed the buildings at the camp and the few cabins on the road leading to it.

"If Reed went all the way down there and only stayed a short time, he had a reason. Maybe the girl is holed up there and he went to check on her. But why would she be there?"

"Can we get an infrared scan of the buildings? That would tell us if anyone is down there."

Jack reached for his cell phone. "Let me see if the director will authorize an IR tech and the equipment. I promised him I'd keep him informed." He started to punch the speed-dial number for the director's direct line and then stopped. "Damn. It's way past five on a Friday. There's no way we can get to him tonight."

"All right. I know a guy that works for a private security outfit, and I believe he has an IR rig. I bet we could get him to do it tonight and tell the director about it tomorrow. What do you think?"

"I think you're nuts and you'll get us both put in jail." Jack shook his head. "But go ahead. Call your man, and let's see what he can do."

# Chapter 19

Friday, 6:15 p.m.

"Please, gentlemen. Mr. Gardner, is everyone here now?" Cal Gardner, the CIA's London station chief, answered yes, and Geoffrey Campbell, the senior MI6 representative called the meeting to order. Deke relaxed in his chair in the conference room of the safe house that MI 6 was using. The house looked like all the others on this side street off Bayswater Road. Two stories with a short flight of steps leading to a basement entrance that was barred shut. The room they were in was painted a pale institutional green that contrasted with the worn off-red linoleum. There were no windows. A steam radiator against the wall hissed and grumbled to itself but provided little heat. He looked around at the people who were seated at the scarred mahogany conference table. The group was small. Besides Gardner and Deke, there were two other Company men and three MI6 agents headed by Campbell, whom Deke knew but had not seen for several years. He wished Patricia and Elizabeth had been allowed to join them, but their superior at MI6 was adamant about their not participating in the bond recovery effort.

Deke and Patricia had parted at Heathrow with a tentative promise to meet again later. She and Elizabeth were taken off to wherever MI6 had its headquarters, and Deke was escorted to the American embassy in Grosvenor Square. He and Gardner had spent a couple of hours going over the events in Karachi and Kohat. Gardner then set up the meeting with Campbell and his MI6 people, and they had lunch in the embassy dining room. They passed the afternoon with teleconferences with Langley. Now he was listening while Gardner brought the British agents up to speed.

"So now we have to decide what we're going to do to get those bonds back from the imam." He turned to Campbell. "I don't suppose we can break down the front door of the mosque and take 'em, can we?"

"Not openly. But there might be a way, a back way, so to speak. We have had that mosque under surveillance for some time. It was originally a town house converted to flats. We have the floor plans. If we could gain entry through the back, we might be able to find the imam and persuade him to give up your bonds."

Deke raised his hand. "If I and one or two others can get in, I'm sure that would be possible." He looked around the table. "Maybe Agent Davis and one of your people could go in with me."

Gardner broke in. "How many people would we face in there, Geoff?"

"There are usually two or three men with the imam. Assistants or bodyguards, we think. But it depends on the time of day. Frequently in the afternoons, there are a half a dozen young men coming and going. We believe it is a training school for terrorists, but we have not confirmed that as yet. Obviously, we don't want to do anything while prayer services are going on." He paused and thought for a moment. "But actually, that might be the best time after all. The faithful have been blocking the street and pavement in front of the building and doing their praying out there for the past few weeks, showing their power to disrupt things as they did in Paris, we believe. The imam usually comes out front and speaks to them from the steps. Perhaps we could use that to our advantage."

Richards, one of the MI6 agents, spoke up. "Could we stage a demonstration in the street at that time? That might provide the cover we need to enter from the back."

Deke grinned. "Particularly if the demonstration got out of hand. It wouldn't have to be a large riot. Just big enough to drive the imam and a couple of his bodyguards back into the mosque. And we would be waiting for them. Could that be done?"

Campbell considered this for a moment or two. "Yes. I think we could stage such a demonstration. We have some people who would like nothing better than to get into a dustup with our friends out there. This will have to be approved by Whitehall, of course." He turned to Cal Gardner. "And I suppose you must contact Langley too."

"Yes, but I don't see a problem. They want the bonds back any way we can get them. That's why they sent Deke over here. He has the right authorization."

One of the MI6 agents stood up. "I suggest that we do this during the *Salat-al-zuhr* prayer time. It will be near midday and will have the biggest crowd in the street outside of the mosque."

"Good point. And that will give us plenty of time to get it organized. MI6 will make the arrangements, and I suggest we meet here at ten tomorrow morning. We will proceed from there. Any further questions, gentlemen?" Campbell looked at each of them in turn, but no one indicated that he had anything else to contribute, so he adjourned the meeting.

Deke, Davis, and Cal Gardner stood on the sidewalk in front of the house. Cal asked, "Will you be ready to act by morning? I'll pass the word to Langley, so they won't be surprised."

Davis nodded, and Deke answered, "I think we're set, Cal. If anything changes, we'll know by ten o'clock, and if we have to, we can adjust things then."

"Okay. Deke, let's find you a hotel room for the night."

They started toward Gardner's car when Deke heard his name called. He looked across the street. Patricia sat in her car opposite the building. He left the others and walked over to her car. "What are you doing here?"

"Waiting for your meeting to end so I could take you to dinner. You haven't eaten yet, have you?"

"No. Hang on a minute." He turned back to Gardner. "You all go on. I'll catch up with you later at the embassy." Turning back to Patricia, he said, "Where are you taking me for dinner?"

She waited until he had gotten into the car before she answered, "My flat. I'm quite a good cook." She grinned at him. "And you can stay there tonight if you want."

Deke took his time but finally said, "Pat, I'll accept the dinner invitation, but Cal has arranged a hotel for me. My bag is at the embassy, and we'll have to swing by there and pick it up."

She pulled out into the quiet street and dropped her left hand onto Deke's leg. "I know. We could get your bag in the morning." She frowned when he shook his head and gently removed her hand.

# Chapter 20

Friday, 9:27 p.m.

Jack and Pete were in Jack's van and headed back to the camp on the Potomac. "The tech will meet us at that bridge on the Potomac, and you can get us back down that road from there. I told you the director thinks we're on a wild-goose chase, but he was willing to let you finish up what you'd started today. I'm not sure he'll like what we're doing now, but maybe he'll go along as long as we don't raise too much dust. He has absolutely forbidden us to do anything else at this point, so even if she is there, we can't go in alone." Jack looked at Pete. "You understand that? He means it. And so do I."

"Okay, boss. I'm cool with it." Pete had explained that Angela had been with him when he tailed Reed to the camp and that he had left her at the Back Yard. Jack was none too pleased that their efforts may have been compromised further, but then he recognized that the girl was a trained FBI agent and probably posed no risk. They had stopped briefly so that Pete could give Angela the keys to his truck with the promise that he would pick it up as soon as he could. She also wasn't happy with the way the day was turning out but realized that she was stuck in Chantilly unless she used his truck to get back to DC.

They had been at the bridge for nearly twenty minutes when the IR technician's unmarked van pulled up. A long-haired young man wearing glasses stepped out and came over to their vehicle. "Hi, Pete." He looked at Jack. "You Frazier?"

Jack answered, "Yeah. Follow us."

When the man was back in his van, Jack pulled out on the blacktop and drove back to the road Pete had shown him. They turned left, bounced over the speed bump-like pile of sand and proceeded slowly through the

79

dark woods. After about fifteen minutes, they came to the brow of the hill leading into the camp area. Jack stopped the van, and Pete got out and went back to the other vehicle. "Larry, can we carry your gear down the hill and get a shot at the buildings from the edge of the woods?"

"Sure. It's only this stuff." The tech indicated two cases about the size of a normal airline carry-on bags. They walked over to the van, and the IR man stuck out his hand to Jack. "I'm Larry Gross by the way."

Jack opened the door so the tech could see the wheelchair. "Glad to meet you. Appreciate your coming out here for us."

Gross eyed the chair and the way the van was rigged so that Jack could handle it. He nodded appreciatively. "Glad to help. I owe Pete a couple of favors." He and Pete returned to his own van.

"Let me give you a hand with that." Pete picked up one of the cases and headed down the hill, keeping well within the trees. Gross followed him with the other case, and they stopped and crouched in the fringe of the woods where they had a good view of the main building. Gross quickly opened one of the cases, which contained a small video screen on an adjustable tripod. He took another piece of camera-like equipment from the other case and plugged the two together with a USB cable. The tech flipped a switch, tapped some keys on the minicomputer built into the case, and watched as a faint outline of the lodge building appeared on the screen. After another switch and a few more taps, a small, very faint, green glow appeared in one corner of the building's outline. "What's that?" Pete spoke quietly.

Gross studied it for a minute. "Looks like someone lying down. But it's really faint. Not putting out normal body heat." He swung the camera-like receiver away from the building, and a bright-green image appeared about twenty yards to the left of it. They watched as it slowly moved away. "That's a deer. See how much more heat it's putting out?" He scanned the building again. The faint glow in the corner was still there.

Pete whispered, "All right. That's all we need to know. Karin's in there."

# Chapter 21

Saturday, 8:30 a.m.

The burly guard showed Gardner, Davis, and Deke into the same conference room at the MI6 safe house. Cal had picked him up at the hotel shortly before seven. He had enjoyed the dinner that Patricia had prepared, and the evening had passed quickly. When he had again refused her offer to let him spend the night at her house, she called a cab for him around nine and kissed him good-bye at the door.

Campbell spoke up when the group had seated themselves, "Gentlemen, everything has been arranged as we discussed last evening. Whitehall has given us their blessing, provided things don't get too messy." He turned to Gardner. "Everything all right with your people?"

"No problem. As I said last night, Deke has all of the right credentials."

"Yes, of course. But now we must be on our way. I will be outside the back entrance with Jameson and Shields. Cal, you and the others will be in front observing the demonstration. You and I will communicate by secure handheld radio. When the proper time arrives, Mitchell and the others will enter the rear of the building. Are there any questions? If not, let us proceed." He led the way from the room.

Two unmarked vans waited for them outside, and the ride to the mosque took just over half an hour in the light Saturday-morning traffic. The teams debarked around the corner from the building and moved to their assigned places. The mosque fronted on Thornton Place, the main street, but there was a back entrance which opened to a small enclosed garden area which could be reached from the adjacent street, Cambert Mews. Deke stayed with the group assembled at the corner of Thornton Place and a cross street while the others moved to the rear of the building and waited behind the garden wall until they were told what was happening out front.

Deke watched as several men entered the street in front of the mosque and began spreading their prayer rugs on the pavement. A policeman had already moved to the intersection at the other end of the block and stopped a small truck from entering. A crowd began to form, and Deke could hear them complaining to the policeman about their rights of free passage being obstructed by the men now beginning to kneel on their prayer rugs. A few men left the crowd by the truck and moved down the sidewalk toward the worshippers and began taunting them. A couple of them pulled out homemade signs and waved them to try to distract the men from their prayers.

Cal spoke quietly, "Looks like Geoff's people showed up right on time. Things should be heating up pretty soon."

A grocer and a tailor talked briefly with one of the protestors on the sidewalk and then went to their shops opposite the mosque. The tailor closed and locked his front door, and the grocer began to take flats of produce from the outside display into his store. The imam and two other men, much younger than he, came out of the mosque and stood on the high front steps. More Muslim men had come into Thornton Place and sat or kneeled on the pavement in front of him. He spoke in Urdu to those who were gathered in the street. A few of the growing crowd of protesters began to shout at the imam, and a couple of them went over to the grocer's and grabbed tomatoes and fruit from the few flats he had left outside. A new group of five tough-looking young men came into the street and began walking down the middle toward the kneeling faithful. Four policemen stood on the sidewalk in front of the tailor shop and watched as fruit and vegetables were thrown at the front of the mosque, and the five toughs began to push their way through the worshippers in the street. Gardner was already talking to Campbell, keeping him informed on the progress of the demonstration. He nodded, and Deke and Agent Davis sprinted for the back of the building. Gardner waited until he saw the imam turn to go back inside and then whispered, "Go. Go," into the radio.

Campbell was waiting for Davis and Deke at the rear door of the mosque. Richards, the MI6 agent, had already jammed a pry bar into the door frame at the site of the deadbolt, and at a nod from his boss, he threw his full weight against it, and the door sprung open. He stepped through and motioned for Deke and Davis to follow. Campbell grabbed

Davis by the arm and pushed another man, a dark-complected Pakistani, forward. Deke recognized him instantly—the newspaper reader from Karachi. Deke stopped and faced Campbell. He pointed at the newcomer and snarled, "Who's that guy, and what the hell is he doing here?"

Campbell shook himself free, "Rahim Aziz, one of our agents from Pakistan. He is your interpreter. Now, get in there."

Deke, Aziz, and Richards burst through the door and into the mosque, running headlong into the imam and his two companions as they headed for the stairway to the second floor. Aziz shouted to them in Urdu, ordering them to get down on the floor. One of the imam's aides reached into his vest for his weapon, and Richards tackled him, knocking him to the floor before he could draw the gun. Deke pointed his Glock at the other man and watched as he and the imam slowly sank to their knees in the hallway. Speaking again in Urdu, Aziz told them they were under arrest and not to resist.

The imam folded his hands in front of his chest and looked up at Aziz. "Why have you done this?" He spoke English.

Aziz turned to Deke, "You do not need a translator. He speaks English. Tell him what you want."

"You are the imam Akbar Hashemi?" Deke held his pistol on the man.

"Yes. That is correct. This is a mosque, and you have defiled it, infidel. Why?"

The man was of average height and appeared to be in his late forties or early fifties. He was thin with a well-trimmed salt-and-pepper beard. Deke motioned for him to stand. "A package of bonds was sent to you from Pakistan. I came to get them." He leaned close to the imam. "And I want them now. Do you understand me?"

The imam shrugged. "And if I do not have such things? What happens then?"

"Don't try to con me. We know they were sent to you." Deke paused. "Faraz told us everything, just before he died." The imam's eyes widened, and Deke went on, "The British authorities may be willing to make a deal with you if you give them up. If you don't cooperate, you're going to spend a long, long time in a British prison. It is your choice. What's it going to be?"

"I do not know anyone named Faraz. And what do you mean, prison?" The imam looked at Deke in disbelief, "I have done nothing wrong. I have broken no English laws."

Deke smiled at him, "You're lying, but I don't think it matters. The people from MI6 know what you've been doing. They believe that you have been running a terrorist training school here in this mosque, and I'm certain they can make that charge stick if they want to." He pushed the man roughly against the wall, "Now let's get serious. We came for the bonds. And we'll get them if we have to take you and this place apart." They could hear police sirens and shouting out front. The demonstration had clearly gotten out of hand.

Imam Akbar Hashemi was silent for a moment. Then he asked, "What sort of arrangement will the British make with me?"

"I can't answer for them. Their man is outside, and he may be able tell you. But first, get me the bonds."

"All right. They are in the office up above, in the safe."

"Let's go." Deke pushed him toward the stairs, and he and Aziz followed him up to the well-appointed office while Richards herded the other two men out the back door. A large safe, the kind usually used for storing weapons, stood against the wall behind an ornate desk.

"Open it." The imam looked at Deke, shrugged, and went to the safe. He punched in the combination, turned the handle, and swung the heavy door open. The left side of the big safe was crowded with rifles. Deke quickly counted six AK-47s, and the same number of M16s with additional long guns, shotguns, and sporting rifles, behind them. Several cartons of ammunition were stacked on the floor of the gun safe. Deke pointed at the open safe. "That will get you a minimum of twenty years if they decide to charge you under the British weapons laws. Where are the bonds?"

"In the file on the shelf to the right. The file is not locked." Akbar Hashemi moved to the desk and collapsed into the chair beside it. "I have failed." He sat quietly, his hands folded in his lap.

Deke pulled the file box from the safe and carried it to the desk. Opening it, he found a large sealed envelope about half the thickness of a ream of copy paper. He held it up. "Are these the bonds?" The imam nodded and stared down at the floor again. Ripping open the flap, Deke saw that he was holding millions of dollars' worth of cashable bearer bonds. "All right, we've got what we came for. Let's get out of here." He took the imam by the arm and raised him from the chair.

Geoff Campbell and his crew met them as they came down into the garden. "Good work, Mitchell." He turned to Richards, his number two.

"Take those others to station C. We'll interrogate them before we turn them over to the home office for disposition. The imam will come with us."

Deke told him about the weapons in the office of the mosque, and Campbell called for additional agents to thoroughly search and secure the building. Then they crowded into the waiting van for the ride back to the MI6 safe house.

They reassembled in the now-familiar conference room. As soon as Gardner arrived, Deke handed the envelope of bonds to him. "There. You can send these back to Langley or do whatever else they want to do with them." He looked around the room at the others. "You are all witnesses. Cal has custody of the bonds." He turned back to Gardner. "Now, let's move on with this so I can get back to DC. But you'd better count them, Cal. I don't think they're all there." The London station chief smiled at him and began counting. After a moment, he shook his head.

"You're right. There's only ten million dollars' worth here." He turned to the imam. "Where are the rest of the bonds?"

Campbell held up his hand. "We'll get to that, I'm sure. We have just a few questions for our friend here." Campbell gestured toward Akbar Hashemi seated at the table. "First, sir, can we offer you anything to make you more comfortable? Tea, perhaps? Or coffee?" The imam shook his head and continued to stare at his hands folded on the table. "Well, then, let's continue." Campbell seated himself opposite this prisoner. Deke sat at the end of the long scarred table next to Rahim Aziz.

Gardner dropped the stack of bonds on the table in front of the imam. "How did these bonds get to you?"

Akbar Hashemi pushed the bonds to one side. "Before I tell you anything more, I want to know what will happen to me now."

Campbell frowned and then said, "I really don't know at this point. From what we saw at the mosque, you have broken a number of our laws and could serve a very long time in our prison system. However, if you cooperate fully, some other arrangement may be made." He looked straight at the imam. "But you must cooperate fully, and we must be satisfied that everything you tell us is the truth and can be verified. Are we in agreement?"

The imam nodded. "Yes. I understand what you are telling me."

Campbell continued, "Good. Now, how did you get the bonds?

"They were sent by courier."

"Really? From Pakistan?"

"Yes. A month ago, I was told that some money for our expenses would come to us by courier. I did not know it would be in this form. I expected bank notes, currency. I did not receive instructions on how I am to convert these papers to something we could use."

"From Pakistan to London by courier. Good. Did you meet this courier?"

"Yes, briefly. When he came to the mosque with the bonds."

"What is his name?"

"I do not know his name. He was referred to as 'Castle' by our people in Pakistan."

Richards handed a folder to Campbell, and he opened it and removed a picture which he handed to the imam. "Is this the man who delivered the package?"

Hashemi studied the photograph for a long minute before he answered, "That could be the man. I only saw him for a short time. I cannot be certain."

Campbell returned the photo to the folder and handed it back to Richards. "Edward Rook. Have him picked up in Islamabad and returned here immediately. We will deal with him then." He turned back to Hashemi. "How many bonds did you receive?"

"Two hundred."

"Um, yes. And apparently there are only one hundred here now. Where are the others?"

"I was instructed to mail them to an address in the United States, and I did so."

Cal Gardner spoke up, "Do you still have that address?"

"Yes. It was a company in San Antonio, Texas."

Cal turned to Deke. "Do we know anything about this?"

"I don't think this has come up before now, but I'm sure we can get to it as soon as I get back there. Jack may have something on it. Remember, there were rumors about a new cell in San Antonio."

"All right. I'll contact Langley and tip them off. Maybe they'll be able to tell you something when you get home. Gardner turned back to Hashemi. "I'll want the name and address of that company."

Aziz leaned close to Deke. "I tried to warn you about Faraz in Karachi. He had been seen with Rook on several occasions in Peshawar and Islamabad."

"Yes. I remember your note. So Faraz was working with the Brits too. Rook must have been his contact there."

"We thought so. Mr. Rook flew to London last Saturday and returned to Islamabad the following day." Aziz shook his head. "He did not contact his superiors at MI6 while he was in London, and he traveled on a false diplomatic passport."

"Did you know he went to the mosque?"

"Yes. Campbell told me he was seen by one of the watchers. But we did not know he was carrying your bonds."

"Well, I guess a diplomatic pouch would be the safest way to transport something like that. No customs check on either end."

Aziz continued, "When he came to Peshawar the other day to meet with the two ladies, we were concerned that he would do something to try and stop you. But you got away to Kohat before he could act. I stayed with him until he met with Wilson, and then I went to the roadblock to wait for your return so we could cover you while you went back to the hotel."

"So that was you in the car at the barricade. Thanks for watching our backs."

"It was no problem. I am sorry we could not have helped Mr. Scott in Kohat. We were one step behind Rook and Faraz at that time."

Geoff Campbell was speaking to the imam again, "After you have given us the names of the men you have been training here, along with a full disclosure of the program, you may be deported. You probably will be able to choose your destination if you cooperate fully. Otherwise, you may be tried as a terrorist and you will spend the rest of your life in one of our maximum-security prisons."

Deke turned to Cal Gardner. "Would our people at Langley like a crack at him before he is deported or jailed? If MI6 wouldn't mind, we could have a team here in a couple of days." He looked at the imam. "Or we could send him to Gitmo or the Farm for a while, or maybe somewhere else."

Gardner nodded. "Good thought, Deke. I'll arrange to have a team sent here. It'll be easier to handle him that way. Less chance of a leak to the press." He turned to Campbell. "You don't have any problems with that, do you, Geoff?"

"No, of course not. We should be through with him in a week or two, and you can have him after that. You have a safe house, I presume."

"Yeah, we have a place that can accommodate him and our team."

Campbell grunted, "I was afraid you would have."

The imam glanced at the stack of bonds on the table. "*Ma Sa Allah.* It is the will of God." He turned to Campbell. "It may not make any difference. If I return to my homeland, I will most likely be executed since I have failed in my mission here."

Campbell looked at him. "Perhaps we could find a country that would offer you asylum."

"It would not matter. I would be found. It is the will of Allah."

Deke spoke up again, "Why don't we turn him? You could let him continue to run his mosque and monitor what goes on there from the inside."

Both Campbell and Gardner looked at him as if he had lost his mind. "What makes you think that this man would work with us without betraying the fact?"

"He knows what the alternative is." He turned to the imam, who was listening to the exchange with a look of wonder on his face. "Do you have a wife? Children?"

"Yes, two wives but only one son so far. Allah has not blessed me with more."

Deke continued, "Why are they not here with you?"

Hashemi shrugged. "My task did not allow it, and we do not have the resources to bring them here."

"It would be a good idea for you to bring them to London when you go back to your mosque. We could arrange for that to happen. No one in your organization would need to know that you have been raided. You should be able to continue to operate pretty much as you did before. With some restrictions, of course." He paused for a moment and then continued, "You do understand that your only alternatives are for us to return you to Pakistan or turn you over to a rendition team. If that happens, you will simply disappear, never to see your wives or son again. Which will it be?"

The imam turned to Campbell. "You would allow this? And arrange to bring my family here?"

Campbell, now convinced that Deke's idea might work, nodded vigorously. "Yes, we could arrange such a thing, after we and Mr. Gardner's people are satisfied that you have cooperated fully during your debriefings."

Hashemi straightened up in his chair. "Sir, I accept your offer, and I will cooperate."

The senior MI6 man stood up. "Good. That's settled then. We'll work out the details as we progress with the debriefings."

Gardner spoke up, "Geoff, if you are through with us for now, we need to get Deke out to Heathrow. He has to get back to Washington tonight."

"Of course." Campbell came around the table and shook hands with his CIA counterpart. Then he turned to Deke. "Mitchell, it was good to see you. Thank you for your help in this matter."

Deke clasped the man's hand. "It was good to meet you again too, sir. Perhaps I'll visit London sometime and look you up."

"Fine, I'd like that." Campbell smiled. "Patricia will know how to reach me."

Deke felt his face redden, and he turned to Gardner. "Let's get out of here, Cal."

Rahim Aziz walked to the door with them. He took Deke's arm. "I would still like to talk with you a bit. I may be in the United States for a short visit in a few weeks. Perhaps we can meet if it is convenient for you."

"Certainly. I'll no longer be with the Agency, but I'll leave some contact information here with Cal if that suits you."

"Perfectly. Have a good flight, my friend." The small man shook Deke's hand and turned away.

"Let's go, Cal."

Gardner hesitated when they got to the waiting car. "Anyone else you need to say good-bye to?"

Deke reached for the car door. "No, we did that last night."

# Chapter 22

Jack Frazier slammed his cell phone down on the desk. "Goddamn it! He's still out of touch." He spun his wheelchair around and faced Pete. "The whole friggin' world could be falling apart, and the director of the CIA and the secretary of defense are out playing goddamn golf!" Pete knew that part of his boss's anger was derived from the fact that he could no longer play the game.

"Jack, we need to get moving on this. Let me go in there and see who is in that lodge."

"No way. Not until we get permission from the man. I don't know if he'll buy our plan even after we get to show him what we've got." He started to reach for the bottom drawer of his desk and then shook his head and stopped. *No. Can't be doing that. Not today,* he thought.

His cell phone buzzed, and he snatched it up, "Frazier."

"Waverly. What's so important that you call me four times on a Saturday morning?

"We're pretty sure we have found Karin Jansen. I need your permission to mount a rescue operation." Jack waited, holding his breath.

"Rescue operation? Are you crazy? Or drunk." Waverly was impatient. "We don't do those kinds of operations here. You know that."

"Yes, sir. But I need to show you what we've found and explain how we can do this. Can we get together soon?"

Waverly took his time answering. "All right. I'm at the Army and Navy Club with the SecDef. Meet me here after lunch. Around two should be about right. If you're in Chantilly, that'll give you enough time to get here."

"All right, sir. We'll be there."

———————

The Army and Navy Club is a very plush, very exclusive establishment catering to the upper echelons of the military and cabinet-grade and near-cabinet-grade civilians. Jack found Ellis Waverly in the smoking room next to the bar. Waverly, seeing that Jack was carrying a large portfolio, moved from the leather easy chair to a small table in the rear of the room. "Is that material classified?" He pointed to the portfolio.

"No, sir. Just some aerial photos and infrared scans. Let me show you what we got last night." Jack spread the photos out and explained that they were pictures of the old government camp. Waverly had never heard of the camp and was unfamiliar with the area. Jack told him that Pete had trailed Reed to the camp and that they had gone there last night and taken IR scans of the lodge building. He showed him the scans and explained what they meant. "Sir, we believe that whoever is lying in the lodge building is Karin Jansen, and we need your approval to go in there and get her."

Waverly fingered the scan photos, "Can you tell if she's dead or alive?"

Jack shook his head. "Not for certain. We spent a couple of hours out there, and there was no movement of the image. But if she were dead, there wouldn't be any heat to respond to the scan. It's faint, but it's there. We believe she's alive. Maybe comatose."

Waverly turned and looked at Frazier. "What's your proposal? You know we can't use military resources for this, or Company people either."

"I guess we were planning on calling the state police or county sheriff out there and telling them what we found, maybe anonymously. They could take it from there."

His boss frowned. "That would raise way too many questions, Jack. But I know some people that may be able to help." He reached for his phone.

# Chapter 23

Saturday, 8:17 p.m.

Deke's flight to Dulles International Airport had landed at 7:34 a.m., and he had cleared customs and immigration by a little after eight o'clock. Pete met him at the gate nearest the VIP exit where Jack was waiting in the van.

"Man, it's good to see you." He hugged Deke and pounded him on the back. "Jack will bring you up to date on what we're going to do about Karin. He did tell you that we found her, didn't he?"

Deke pushed the big man off and reached for the door of the van. "Yeah, but no details." He climbed into the front seat next to his boss. "Jack. Thanks. What do we do tonight?"

"Nothing tonight. We're still waiting for Waverly to finish setting up something with the West Virginia State Police." Frazier shook his head a little. "The man has connections. I was with him when he called the commander over there and explained what we wanted. The guy promised to dig up some people and let Waverly know when and where we could meet them and go after Karin. It shouldn't have taken this long, but even state cops have to go through the bureaucratic hoops, I guess."

"Bullshit. If you know where she is, let's just go get her." Deke was in no mood to delay rescuing the woman whom he now knew he loved and wanted to marry.

"Deke, I'm sorry, but we just can't do that without Waverly's say-so. Just be patient for a little longer." He grabbed Deke by the arm. "I'm sure we'll get the word soon. We'll go out to Chantilly and wait for his call at the office."

By nine o'clock, the three of them were settled in Jack's office. Deke brought them up to date on the events in Pakistan and London. Jack had queried Langley about the possible connection between the bonds going missing in Pakistan and then being delivered to an electronics wholesaler in San Antonio, but there was no further information available. During his flight, Deke remembered that Karin had been going to interview people at a company in that city. He told Jack and Pete everything he knew about her intentions.

"If that's the same outfit, then there may be a reason why she was kidnapped. If that's really what happened to her . . ." Jack paused. "But what does Tom Reed have to do with it?" He poured each of them a solid shot of his favorite bourbon and now took a sip from his glass.

Deke shook his head and shrugged. "It doesn't make much sense. If the AG's office was investigating this company, what were they looking for? Certainly not a national security threat. That's the FBI's area."

Jack's cell phone buzzed, and he grabbed it from the desk top. "Frazier."

"Waverly. The West Virginia State Police will have some people at the road to that camp at eight o'clock tomorrow morning. You are not to do anything until you connect with them. Is that understood?"

Jack grimaced and answered, "Yes, sir. I understand. But can't we get it done tonight?"

"No. They have no resources available until tomorrow morning." The director's tone softened. "Sorry, Jack, but that's the best I could do. Good luck."

"Eight o'clock in the morning at the road to the camp. There's nothing we can do tonight."

Deke swore and pounded his fist on the desk. "She could be dead by tomorrow morning." He finally realized that he wanted to spend the rest of his life with Karin, whether it was in Washington, DC, or in south Texas. It didn't matter anymore. He loved her.

Jack drained his glass. "Deke, let's get you home, so you can get some sleep. We'll have to meet here about five to get out there in time."

Pete stood up. "I'll take you home and pick you up in the morning." He finished his drink too and put the glass on the desk.

"All right. Let's go. I guess I could use a little sleep." Deke left his bourbon untouched. "It's been a busy week."

# Chapter 24

Sunday, 7:39 a.m.

Karin was wide awake when the four men came into the room. She looked straight at Tom Reed. "You've been here before." Her mouth and throat were so dry that her words were barely intelligible. She moistened her lips as best she could and tried again. "Tom, what's going on? Why have you done this?" An older man, much larger than Tom Reed, moved to the bedside. She couldn't name him, but he looked vaguely familiar. The other two men stood back, and she knew that she had never seen either of them.

The big man spoke, "Get the handcuffs off. We need to get out of here." When Reed didn't move, the man shoved him toward the bed. "Dammit, I said get 'em off—now."

Reed still hesitated but then went to the foot of the bed and fumbled with the key to the cuff that held Karin's ankle. As soon as he released it, she kicked at him as hard as she could. He was slow in reacting, and her foot grazed his head, knocking him backward. She kicked at him again and tried to swing around to a sitting position on the edge of the bed, but she was so weak that she could barely make the movement. One of the two men in the shadows snickered, "You brought us all the way from Philly to take care of this little thing. I think you could have finished her off yourself."

Chilton snarled, "Shut up. I'm not paying you to think." He turned to Reed again. "Get the other cuff off, and let's get her out to the car."

Karin swung her free hand at Reed as he came close.

He stepped back again. "Karin, I'm trying to help you. Please don't fight us." His voice was pleading.

"Why?" she croaked. "What have I done? What's this all about, Tom?" She fell back on the bed again, exhausted by her efforts. *Who are these others, and what are they going to do with me? I'm so lost. There must be a way out.*

Reed unfastened the other handcuff. Warily he reached for her to help her sit up, but she didn't attempt to hit him again. He turned to Chilton, "I don't think she can walk. She's awfully weak."

"It doesn't matter." He motioned to the others. "Pick her up, and carry her if you have to."

They came forward, and each took an arm, hoisting Karin to her feet. "C'mon, lady. We're going to take a little trip. Just the three of us."

She hung limply in their grasp. She was weak but was deliberately making herself a deadweight. *I won't help them at all. Maybe there's someplace I can run when we get out of this room. God, I wish I knew where we were.* They lifted her just enough so that her feet didn't touch the floor, and began walking toward the door. She heard the big man ordering Reed to get her purse and "all that other crap you brought up here." *I wish I knew who he was. He's the one giving orders and making decisions. Maybe I can talk to him.* They were in a bigger room now, and she could see that it was some sort of hunting lodge. It was light enough that she could see the outlines of furniture draped with protective coverings. *Okay, an abandoned lodge. But where is it?* The big man was in front of them now and heading for the main door. Through the window she could see two cars parked outside, Tom's white Mercedes and a dark sedan of some other make. "Wait," she said. "You're hurting my arms. Give me a minute, please."

The two men stopped and let her feet down to the floor, but they still held her arms. She looked at the big man. "I'm sure I know you from somewhere. Who are you, and why are you making Tom do this?'

The man smiled. "Oh, we've met, Miss Jansen." There was no humor in his smile. "In a few more hours, it won't matter anyway. You'll be long gone, and we won't have to worry about you anymore." He waited a moment and then continued, "My name is Robert Chilton, and I work for Senator Whiting. Do you remember me now? And, just for the record, I'm not making Tom do anything. He's doing everything of his own accord. Isn't that right, Tom?" He turned to the door again. "Now, let's get out of here."

*Now it's beginning to make sense. The Whiting investigation. But why just me? Tom's involved in the inquiry too. Oh God, it must be true, and he's in on it.* She tried to think of something she could say or do but couldn't come up with anything that would help. *What are they going to do with me?* Then she realized that she knew too much and that the two men holding her were probably going to kill her. *It's over. I'm going to die. Oh Deke, I wish I had told you that I love you.* She tried to twist away from them, but they held her arms too tightly, and she slumped between them.

# Chapter 25

Sunday, 8:00 a.m.

The big West Virginia State Police lieutenant removed his "Smokey Bear" hat and ran his fingers through his crew-cut hair. "Sir, we should have two more cars here within the next fifteen minutes. We'll be ready to go down to the camp then." He paused for a minute and looked closely at Deke and Pete. "You're absolutely certain that the girl is in that old lodge building?"

Pete nodded. "Friday night we confirmed that there is someone in there, and we believe it is Karin Jansen, the woman who's missing."

"All right. As soon as the other officers get here, we'll block this road and go on down there." He turned away from Jack's van and walked back to his patrol car.

Pete leaned against the driver's side door of the van and bent down to look in at Jack. "I didn't know you had pull with the state patrol over here. I'll remember that the next time I get busted for speeding."

Jack laughed. "Doesn't work that way. The director pulled the strings on this one. And your tickets are your own problem."

"You're sure Karin's in there?" Deke stood in front of the van.

Pete turned to face Deke. "Yeah. Gross and I ran a half a dozen scans on that building from all angles, and he swears that the IR image is someone lying down in that room. You saw the printouts of the images. I can't think of anyone or anything else it could be. We need to get in there and get her out. She could have been in that room since Monday night if that's where Reed took her."

Jack nodded. "Okay. As soon as the rest of the troopers get here, you two can go in."

Less than ten minutes later, two more patrol cars pulled up. One, with two officers, remained on the county road, and the other, along with the lieutenant's car and with Jack's van leading, proceeded down the road to the camp.

They came out of the woods at the crest of the hill that overlooked the camp area, and Pete exploded, "Christ, that's Reed's car down there!"

Jack squeezed the accelerator control, and they careened down the hill, swerving to a stop in front of the white Mercedes. Deke and Pete scrambled out of the van just as the door of the lodge opened, and Robert Chilton stepped onto the porch. The two police cars were now also in front of the lodge, and troopers were spilling out of them, with guns drawn. Deke's own Glock was in his hand, and he yelled, "Freeze! This is the police!"

Chilton jumped back into the lodge and slammed the door. The two thugs from Philadelphia dropped Karin like a bag of potatoes and looked for another way out of the room. Dumbstruck, Reed stood absolutely still for a minute and then bolted for the kitchen, dropping Karin's laptop and purse. He knew there was a backdoor there. Chilton turned in time to see him go through the door. He shouted, "Come back here, you little bastard!" Reed didn't stop. In the kitchen, he tried the door but couldn't budge it. Realizing that it had a padlock on the outside, he turned to the window over the sink. Using a garbage can, he smashed the window and pushed his way through. Outside, he hesitated a second or two and then began to run toward the river which he knew was only a few hundred yards away through the woods.

Out front, Deke and Pete heard the window break and ran for the corner of the building. They saw a man running for the trees. Pete slapped Deke on the shoulder. "That's Reed. Get him."

# Chapter 26

Sunday, 8:25

Chilton moved toward the door. He shouted, "I'm coming out. I'm unarmed."

"Bullshit. I'm not giving up." The smaller of the two thugs pulled his pistol from his waistband and smashed the front window with its butt. Sticking his arm out, he looked for a target.

Pete had climbed the porch rail from the end and was flattened against the lodge wall next to the window when it suddenly broke. He grabbed the arm that appeared and, with one heave, pulled the man through the window and onto the porch. The thug landed on his stomach, and Pete pinned him to the boards with a knee in his back, putting his full weight on the man. He jerked the gun from the surprised hit man's hand. One of the troopers came to Pete's aid and handcuffed the would-be killer who was now gasping for breath. Pete stood and looked to the door as Chilton stepped through.

"Hands on your head. Get on your knees." The lieutenant's orders were clear.

Chilton stood with his hands at his sides. "Young man, do you know who I am?"

"No. And I don't care who you think you are. If you're not on your knees in two seconds, I'll shoot you for resisting arrest. Now hit the floor!" The officer came up to the porch steps, and Chilton reluctantly got down on his knees and placed his hands on his head. Another trooper quickly shoved his arms down behind his back and handcuffed him, making sure the cuffs were tight enough to hurt.

Pete and the lieutenant went through the door into the lodge and found Karin lying on the floor. "Karin. It's Pete Saunders. Are you hurt?"

She shook her head, "No. There's another man." She waved her arm toward the back of the lodge room.

"Take care of her." Pete headed for a hallway that appeared to lead to other rooms. He dropped to one knee and looked carefully around the door frame. There were three doors, all closed, in the short hall. He moved cautiously to the first one on the left and tried the knob. It was locked. The second door was on the right, and it too was locked. He went to the last door at the end of the hall and kicked it open.

The two gunshots were nearly simultaneous, but Pete's aim was truer. The second man collapsed against the sink in the small bathroom, with Pete's bullet in his chest.

The lieutenant glanced into the room. "Good shot. You all right?"

Pete lowered his pistol and eased the hammer down. "Yeah." He looked at the hole in the sleeve of his shirt and felt the sting of the bullet that had creased him. "He missed by a mile."

# Chapter 27

Sunday, 8:45 a.m.

The woods were patchy thick with open areas scattered here and there. Reed moved through them without worrying about how much noise he was making. He just wanted to put some distance between himself and whatever was happening back at the lodge. He didn't know whether anyone had seen him when he went out of the kitchen window, but he didn't think he'd been spotted.

The ground rose steeply to the southwest as it neared the river, and Reed was having trouble keeping up his pace. He was in reasonably good condition, but this was not something he was used to doing. He wasn't the outdoor type. He stopped to catch his breath and heard gunshots from the direction of the lodge. *God, now what have we done. Those were police back there. Who would be stupid enough to get in a gunfight with them? Probably those idiots Robert brought down from Philadelphia.* He listened for another moment, but there were no more shots. Then he thought he heard something moving in the brush below him on the hill. *Is someone following me? I didn't see anyone when I got away from the lodge. Don't panic. Just get to the river and follow it up to the bridge.* He was trying to form a plan now. He knew if he could get to the highway, he could probably get a ride and get away from the area. *But then what will I do? Karin knows what we did. Maybe I'd be better off if I went back. No, just get someplace safe and think it through.* He started climbing again and had only gone a few yards when he heard rocks clatter down the slope behind him. *There is someone after me.*

Deke slipped and dislodged some small stones when he caught himself. *Damn. Got to be more careful. Don't want to panic him and make him do something stupid. Just trail him and take him down when the time comes.* He managed to stay out of sight whenever Reed stopped and looked back. Reed was only thirty yards ahead of him on the steep slope and was stopping to rest more frequently now. *All right. That's far enough. Time to end this thing.* Deke eased the Glock out of its holster and sighted carefully on a rock ten feet to the left of his quarry. He squeezed off a round and saw dust and broken shale burst from his target. Reed whirled around, lost his footing and fell on his back, sliding a half-dozen feet down the slope.

"Stay where you are, Reed. I'm coming up to you."

———

*Oh Christ, that's Mitchell. He'll kill me for what I've done to Karin.* Reed scrambled to his feet and started back up the hill. When he got to the top and turned toward the river, he saw that he was only a few feet from the edge of the cliff. It was a sheer drop of two hundred feet to the shallow water and rocks below. He was trapped.

———

Deke crested the hill and faced Reed. He walked slowly toward the man and stopped twenty feet in front of him, with the Glock held loosely in his right hand.

"Don't do anything foolish, Tom. I don't want to have to shoot you." He kept his voice calm even though he was shaking with rage. *Make a move so I can kill you, you bastard. I don't know what all you've done to Karin, but I will kill you for it if you give me an excuse.* Deke took a couple of steps toward Reed. "Come on, now. We're going back down to the lodge, and you're going to give yourself up to the police. Do you understand me?"

"Kidnapping is a federal offense. I'll go to prison for that." Tears coursed down his cheeks. "I can't go back." He stepped closer to the edge and looked down at the river. *I could jump and end it,* he thought. *Or I could make him shoot me. Suicide by CIA.* He smiled to himself. *What a headline that would make.* Suddenly, he found himself flat on his back with Deke's foot on his chest. Deke had moved swiftly and grabbed him from behind, throwing him to the ground well clear of the edge of the cliff.

"I said we're going back." Deke rolled him over and stripped Reed's belt from its loops. He pulled the now docile man to his feet and secured his wrists behind his back with the belt. "Now, let's not have any more trouble. Move." He shoved Reed down the hill in the direction of the lodge.

# Chapter 28

Sunday, 9:20 a.m.

They met the state police lieutenant and one of the troopers about halfway to the lodge. Deke turned Reed over to the trooper and asked the lieutenant, "How's Karin? Is she all right?"

"She doesn't seem to be hurt. Just very weak. We've called for a chopper and EMT's. We need to get her to a hospital."

"Where's the nearest major one?"

"That would be Martinsburg or maybe Winchester. We'll let the EMT's decide when they get here."

The helicopter arrived before they got back to the lodge. The EMTs had already put Karin on a gurney and were bringing her out of the building. Deke stopped them and took her hand. She opened her eyes and, recognizing him, squeezed his hand as hard as she could. He could barely feel the pressure.

"Karin, I love you." Tears welled up in Deke's eyes, and he turned his head away so that she wouldn't see. "You're—we're going to be okay. I promise you." He squeezed her hand and, bending down, kissed her. "I'll see you at the hospital." He stepped back, and the EMTs hurried to load the gurney. Pete came up beside him, and they watched the helicopter take off.

Jack called to them, and they went over to the van. "I've been on the phone with the director, so he knows what happened here this morning." The lieutenant came up as he was speaking, and Jack turned to him. "We're leaving the rest of this to you. You've got three perps in custody and a lot of evidence to take care of, so we'll get out of your hair. It's not our business anyway." He looked the officer straight in the eye. "I think your commander will tell you that we weren't even here. You okay with that?"

The young man reached out to shake hands with Jack and then with Pete and Deke in turn. "Yes, sir. I'm sure my commander will have an interesting story for the press conference, if there is one." He saluted and turned away.

"All right. Let's get to the hospital."

# Chapter 29

Saturday, 2:15 p.m.

Karin was sitting on the couch in her living room with Deke next to her while Pete lounged in the big, matching easy chair and Jack was parked in his wheelchair on the other side of the coffee table. She had been released from the hospital the day before. Her six-day stay in Winchester had been unremarkable. The doctors figured out which drugs she had been given and counteracted them quickly. Phenobarbital can become addictive, but Karin hadn't been given enough of it to cause a problem. Nevertheless, they monitored her closely. The GHB had run its course and was not of concern. Bed rest, food, and IV fluids for six days had restored her physically, but it would take some time for the anxiety and bad dreams to go away. Deke had brought her home from the hospital and stayed the night with her, watching as she slept restlessly, occasionally crying out softly. Pete had been a constant visitor to her room in the hospital in Winchester, and now that she was home again, Jack was on hand to see that she was being well taken care of.

Pete twisted the top from his second bottle of Alaskan Amber beer and poured it into his glass. "When's Reed's trial begin, Jack? This week?"

Frazier looked up from his glass of bourbon. "No, not until the twenty-fifth. He and Chilton will go to court the same day." He took a sip of his drink. "I think they'll both be convicted and probably go down hard." He looked at Karin. "It'll be your testimony that will put them away on the kidnapping charge. I think they'll also be charged with conspiracy to commit murder. I heard that the goon from Philadelphia that Pete manhandled sang like a canary. Chilton's going to get tagged for that. Reed was just an accessory."

Karin sighed, "Poor Tom. He just didn't know what he was getting into."

Deke took her hand. "Maybe not. But he made his own choices all along the way. I doubt that even Chilton had any idea about where that promised campaign contribution was coming from. Talk about bizarre."

Jack took another swallow from his glass and then put a fresh ice cube into it. "Yeah. The director tells me that the outfit in Texas had been set up as a front for that al-Qaeda cell since way before 9/11. One of my sources told me that when the FBI busted them last Tuesday, they found all sorts of plans and computer stuff that tied them to the attacks on the towers and the Pentagon. By the way, the rest of the bonds were there, delivered by the US mail." He continued, "I think Senator Whiting is going to go down too. Whether he knew anything about what Chilton and Reed were doing or not, the Senate is going to go after him. The least he'll get is a censure, and he'll probably be forced to resign, for health reasons, I would assume."

"You and the director getting pretty chummy, boss?" Pete's question verged on insubordination, but he asked it with a smile.

Jack took a big swallow of his drink this time. "I suppose you two have already guessed that I'm leaving RECOM." They both nodded. "The man offered me a job I can't refuse." He paused. "I have to be in Mexico City by the first of the year. We're opening a station there, and I'm going to be the chief."

Pete jumped up and grabbed Jack's hand. "Man, that's great. And I thought you were going to retire." He stopped. "So who's going to take over RECOM?"

Jack turned and looked at Deke. "Did you accept his offer?"

Nodding, Deke turned to Karin. "I couldn't refuse either."

She pulled away from him, her blue eyes flashing. "And when were you going to tell me this?"

"Just before I asked you to marry me, like right now." Deke took both of her hands in his. "I love you, Karin. Will you marry me?"

She pulled her hands away and then threw her arms around his neck and kissed him. "I know you do. And I love you. Yes, I'll marry you." She laughed. "When?"

Deke kissed her again and said, "How about we go to Michigan to see your folks at Thanksgiving and get married there? Jack can hold the fort for a couple of months before he goes south. The director told me I could have whatever time off I needed to take care of you and a few other things."

Karin nodded and hugged him again.

Jack coughed. "Well, I'm glad we got all that settled." He refilled his glass and said, "Here's to the newly engaged. Congratulations and cheers."

They all drank to the toast.

Pete reached for another bottle of beer, and Jack spoke up again. "Whatever happened to Angela, Pete?"

"Oh, didn't I tell you? She was the one who tipped the AG's office about the fingerprints and our interest in Tom Reed. Said she thought we were overstepping our bounds. Domestic surveillance is an FBI prerogative, and she didn't think the CIA should be doing it." He took a swallow of his beer. "Got her promoted early and bumped to a field office." He smiled. "But I think our director had a hand in that. She left for Fairbanks on Thursday." He took a drink of his beer. "Serves her right. I hear the winters are brutal up there."